One Night A Week

Book by
Richard Harris
Lyrics by
Mary Stewart-David
Music by
Denis King

Based on the play *Stepping Out*
by Richard Harris
Americanization by
Astrid Ronning & Nina Seely

A SAMUEL FRENCH ACTING EDITION

SAMUEL FRENCH

FOUNDED 1830

NEW YORK HOLLYWOOD LONDON TORONTO

SAMUELFRENCH.COM

RENTAL MATERIALS

An orchestration consisting of **Piano/Conductor's Score, Piano/Keyboards 1 & 2, Trumpet, Woodwinds 1 & 2, Guitar,** and **Percussion**, will be loaned two months prior to the production ONLY on the receipt of the Licensing Fee quoted for all performances, the rental fee and a refundable deposit.

Full orchestral backing tracks on CD, with additional vocal guide track are also available.

Please contact Samuel French for perusal of the music materials as well as a performance license application.

IMPORTANT BILLING AND CREDIT
REQUIREMENTS

All producers of *ONE NIGHT A WEEK must* give credit to the Authors of the Play in all programs distributed in connection with performances of the Play, and in all instances in which the title of the Play appears for the purposes of advertising, publicizing or otherwise exploiting the Play and/or a production. The names of the Authors *must* appear on a separate line on which no other name appears, immediately following the title and *must* appear in size of type not less than fifty percent of the size of the title type.

ONE NIGHT A WEEK was first performed at the Theatre Royal, Plymouth under the title *Stepping Out - The Musical* and subsequently presented by Bill Kenwright in association with The Churchill Theatre, Bromley and Tyne Theatre and Opera House, Newcastle, at the Albery Theatre (now the Noel Coward), London, on October 8th, 1997. The performance was directed by Julia McKenzie, with sets by Sean Cavanagh, sound by Terry Jardine, musical direction by Stephen Hill, choreography by Tudor Davies and Miranda Fellows. The cast was as follows:

MAVIS (TINA) . . . . Liz Robertson

SYLVIA (SHELLEY) . . . . Helen Bennett

ROSE . . . . Sharon D. Clarke

DOROTHY . . . . Helen Cotterill

ANDY . . . . Felicity Goodson

VERA (VIVIENNE) . . . . Carolyn Pickles

LYNNE . . . . Rachel Spry

GEOFFREY . . . . Colin Wakefield

MRS. FRASER . . . . Gwendolyn Watts

MAXINE . . . . Barbara Young

CHARACTERS

TINA is an ex-pro dancer, attractive, in her late 30s. She wears a T-shirt, tights, leg warmers, old scuffed tap shoes, and a man's sweater tied around her shoulders.

MRS. FRASER is in her late 50s, a square-shaped no-nonsense Mid-Westerner who prides herself on her pessimism. She wears a wool coat, knit hat, and clumpy shoes, and can usually be seen gnawing on some kind of fresh fruit.

SHELLEY is in her early 30s, short, blonde, and bubbly. Her bright and outrageous clothing accentuates her ample curves. She wears grubby old white sneakers and chews gum most of the time.

MAXINE is a good-looking 40-something. She has dyed hair and good make-up. She wears a tight red leotard over a black turtleneck, long red legwarmers and old, soft tap shoes. There are big rocks on her fingers.

DOROTHY is small, anxious and bird-like, could be anywhere from 30 to 50. She wears black shiny tap shoes, a black leotard, and has an ace support bandage around one knee. There is a hint of white cotton underpants showing under the leotard.

LYNNE is 19. She is eager to please, has a lovely face, but is of large proportions. She never wears make-up and her skin glows healthily. She wears tights, a cardigan which matches her legwarmers, and scuffed tap shoes.

ROSE is a large, black woman of Caribbean extraction, in her 40s, wearing an obvious wig, a bright pink dress over black tights, and white tap shoes with mismatched shoelaces. She has large strings of beads around her neck and lots of rings on her fingers.

ANDY is tall, thin, and in her mid-30s. She wears a long cardigan over a plain dress, and new tap shoes. She is inclined to stoop as if ashamed of her height.

VIVIENNE is in her mid-30s, neat and proper and perfectly groomed. She wears an expensive belted trench coat, high heels, and carries a good leather bag. Her dyed red hair and make-up are immaculate. But for all her primness, she dresses in a way that suggests the high-class tart.

GEOFFREY is tall, in his mid-40s. He is the kind of man who doesn't like being noticed, and most of the time isn't. He wears cheap tap shoes.

SETTING

The main setting is the gym in an old YMCA community center in Suburbia, USA. It is a high-ceilinged room with a scuffed wooden floor on which faded lines define a basketball court. Most of the rear wall is taken up by a large window covered with protective mesh, below which is a small proscenium stage with steps leading up to it, piled with clutter from other community activites (i.e. boxes of children's musical instruments, arts & crafts items, assorted gym and sports equipment, old scenery left over from amateur productions, etc.) There are doors to either side of the stage, leading through to the unseen dressing rooms. Downstage right a pair of swinging doors lead to the lobby, seen later in the play. Left of the stage are a pair of double doors which are marked FIRE EXIT. Folding chairs are set randomly along each of the walls, which are dotted with with the usual safety notices, children's art displays, etc. Downstage left is an elderly upright piano and stool with a cushion. On the piano is a juice carton, an apple core, a small cash box and a spiral bound ledger. Personal bags, coats and shoes are scattered on and around the chairs. The "fourth wall" is the unseen practice mirror.

A NOTE ON THE MUSIC

For producers without access to musicians or an orchestra, please know that full orchestral backing tracks, with additional vocal guide track are available on CD for use in performance and rehearsal. Please contact Samuel French at SamuelFrench.com for more information on how to obtain these materials.

MUSICAL NUMBERS

ACT 1

Overture

One Night A Week. . . . . **TINA** & **COMPANY**

One Night A Week (reprise) . . . . .On Stage Piano

Right . . . . **ANDY** & **GEOFFREY**

Don't Ask Me . . . .**ROSE** & **COMPANY**

Love To. . . . . **LYNNE** & **DOROTHY**

What Do Men Think?. . . . . **SHELLEY, ROSE, MAXINE, DOROTHY**

Too Much . . . . **TINA**

Never Feel The Same Again . . . .**ANDY** & **GEOFFREY**

Definitely You . . . .**VIVIENNE** & **COMPANY**

One Night A Week (reprise) . . . .**TINA** & **COMPANY**

ACT II

Entr'acte

Doctor Footlights . . . .**MAXINE, SHELLEY, VIVIENNE, LYNNE, DOROTHY**

Right (Reprise) . . . . **GEOFFREY**

Just The Same. . . . . **MAXINE**

What I Want. . . . . **SHELLEY, ROSE, MAXINE, DOROTHY, TINA**

Once More . . . .**TINA** & **LYNNE**

Too Much (reprise) . . . . **TINA**

Loving Him . . . . **VIVIENNE, ANDY, TINA**

Stepping Out. . . . .**COMPANY**

ACT ONE

(The overture rises to an unfulfilled climax. A pause, followed by a few bars of introduction thumped out heavily and irritably on a piano. There is a moment's silence, then the few bars are repeated.)

MRS. FRASER. *(from behind the curtain)* Are we starting or aren't we?

(The curtain slowly rises.)

Scene One

(The YMCA Gym. An evening in February.)

*(**MAXINE**, **LYNNE**, **ANDY** and **DOROTHY** stand in a line downstage, regarding themselves with varying degrees of affection in the unseen mirror. **GEOFFREY** is upstage with one foot on a chair, tying his shoelace. **MRS. FRASER** sits at the piano, glowering. **TINA** enters briskly through the swinging doors, tosses her cigarettes and lighter down on the piano, takes a slurp from a can of Coke sitting there with a straw in it, and turns, as **MRS. FRASER** distastefully relegates **TINA**'s pack of cigarettes to the metal wastebasket by the piano.)*

TINA. Okay everyone.

*(There is a flurry of movement. **SHELLEY** is hurrying out of the dressing room.)*

SHELLEY. *(calling back)* Come on – we're startin'!

(She jumps down heavily from the stage steps, clutching her ample bosom.)

I gotta stop doin' that. *(She moves to join the others.)*

TINA. Where's Rose?

SHELLEY. One of her shoe laces broke.

MAXINE. *(calls)* Step on it, Rose – we're waiting!

DOROTHY. Waiting – yes.

LYNNE. Sh' I go get her, Tina?

TINA. No, it's all right, Lynne, she can jump in when she's ready...Okay then! Let's do it. Geoffrey, scoot yourself into the middle now where we can see you... *(She takes a last slurp from her Coke can.)* Whenever you're ready, Glenda.

*(**GEOFFREY** somewhat unwillingly moves into the center of the line, nudged by **SHELLEY** and winked at by **MAXINE** as **TINA** moves to face out front, her back to the class.)*

We'll start with some nice relaxing...four bends... yeah...warm those knees...and ankles...and the other side...that's it....and toe-taps...remember this?

*(And they begin the simple warm-up routine with **MRS. FRASER** playing in very strict tempo.)*

*(**LYNNE** is good, light on her feet and attentive. She smiles a lot but bites a nail when she does something wrong. She's very serious about dancing.)*

*(**DOROTHY** makes extravagantly large movements, is unsmiling and looking all the time at **TINA**'s feet.)*

*(**MAXINE** is confident, competent, and enjoying it. She's the best mover in the group, the most natural dancer and, unlike most of them, uses her arms well.)*

*(**ANDY** has no co-ordination whatsoever. She looks dog-gedly to the front as though trying to suggest that she really isn't here, keeps her arms tight to her sides and her fists clenched. She raises her feet as though avoiding dog doo.)*

*(**GEOFFREY** is limited but competent. When he smiles – for instance at a comment on someone else's mistake – it's as though he's forgotten himself and is quick to control it.)*

(**SHELLEY** *chews gum, isn't very good and doesn't give a damn. She's always that little bit out of step: if the others do something to the left, she's guaranteed to do it to the right.*)

(*As they dance,* **TINA** *will dance along with them, smiling and calling out the steps, instructing them via the mirror. She seems to be enjoying it. After all, they come here to have a good time, and she's a pro whose job is to make the customers happy.*)

TINA. *(cont.)* Okay and let's do it again but spread out you guys, you're all bunched up…there you go, and don't look so serious, Andy, you're here to enjoy yourself. Look in the mirror and five six seven eight…

"ONE NIGHT A WEEK"

ONE NIGHT A WEEK IT'S TIME TO LET GO
ONE NIGHT A WEEK START TAPPING THAT TOE
YOU MAY FEEL TIRED AND COLD
YOU MAY BE READY TO FOLD
MAYBE YOU FEEL YOUR NERVES
ARE FRAYED AND BRITTLE
SO LOOSEN IT UP A LITTLE

ONE NIGHT A WEEK

MRS. FRASER.
TWO THREE

TINA.
IT'S TIME TO HAVE FUN

MRS. FRASER. *(aside)*
YEAH IT'S A LAUGH A MINUTE

TINA.
THAT'S WHY WE'RE HERE

MRS. FRASER.
NOT ME

TINA.
WHEN ALL'S SAID AND DONE

MRS. FRASER.
AT LEAST THERE'S SOME MONEY IN IT

TINA.

THIS IS YOUR MOMENT TO SHINE
GO FIND YOUR PLACE IN THE LINE
AND CREATE SOMETHING THAT IS QUITE UNIQUE

MRS. FRASER.

WELL THAT'S ONE WORD FOR IT

TINA.

JUST FOR A WHILE

MRS. FRASER.

THANK GOD

TINA.

YOU'LL FIND THERE'S A REASON TO SMILE

MRS. FRASER.

IT'S ONLY

TINA.

ON

BOTH.

ONE NIGHT A WEEK

(**MRS. FRASER** *will vamp as* **TINA** *demonstrates via the mirror and the others copy her with varying degrees of competence as*)

TINA. Okay, here's what we're going to do: it's four flaps and tap step ball change followed by a cramp roll starting with your left foot…no, Shelley your left foot…no, your other left foot.

SHELLEY. I can't think and move at the same time – it's not natural.

TINA. Well try it anyway.

(**ROSE** *hurries out of the dressing room to join the line. Her white tap shoes are tied with one short black lace and one long white one. She has little sense of rhythm but loves every minute of it. Almost as soon as she starts dancing, she will be hopping on one leg and rubbing the other calf.*)

TINA. Good evening Rose, glad you could join us.

ROSE. Sorry Tina, problem with my laces.

TINA. So I see – and it's…

MRS. FRASER.
ONE NIGHT A WEEK

TINA. Three four

MRS. FRASER.
IT'S ALWAYS THE SAME

TINA. Oh Rose, don't tell me your leg's going numb already?

MRS. FRASER.
HERE'S WHAT YOU GET

ROSE. I don't know, I can't feel it.

MRS. FRASER.
THE HALT AND THE LAME
LOOK – YOU CAN SEE AT A GLANCE
WATCHING THE WAY THAT THEY DANCE
NONE OF'EM COME DOWN HERE TO STUDY RHYTHM
AND WHY IS THAT MAN –

TINA. Nice, Geoffrey!

MRS. FRASER.
IN WITH 'EM?
ONE NIGHT A WEEK

TINA. Five six

MRS. FRASER.
THEY PUFF AND THEY BLOW

TINA. Not so big, Dorothy…nice and small

MRS. FRASER.
WHY THEY PERSIST

DOROTHY. Small – yes.

MRS. FRASER.
I'M DARNED IF I KNOW

TINA. Better, much better

MRS. FRASER.
MAYBE AEROBICS IS FULL
COULD IT BE HIM THAT'S THE PULL
MAYBE THEY DREAM OF DANCING CHEEK TO CHEEK

TINA. Good…GOOD….*GOOD*!

MRS. FRASER.
> SEEMS LIKE A DREAM
> THAT'S LIKELY TO RUN OUT OF STEAM
> ON ONE NIGHT A WEEK

(Music continues as **TINA** *leads the class upstage.* **MAXINE** *is left admiring herself in the mirror. Later,* **SHELLEY**, **DOT** *and* **LYNNE** *will join her during:)*

TINA. Andy – try to keep the weight on the balls of your feet...no, your heels on the floor but the weight on your toes, okay?

DOROTHY. On your toes – yes...

MAXINE. Like this, sweetie. *(She demonstrates for* **ANDY** *as:)*

TINA. And you're all still being kind of heavy – try to keep it nice and light, nice and light – and Shelley – try to keep your knees together.

SHELLEY. I've been tryin' to keep my knees together all my life.

MAXINE. Haven't we all, darling?
> IN THE MIRROR
> FIRM AND HARD
> FILLING OUT
> A LEOTARD
> SO THE EYES
> COULD USE A TUCK

SHELLEY.
> AND THE THIGHS
> A LIPOSUCK

LYNNE/DOT./MAX/SHEL.
> WITH THE LYCRA
> SMOOTH AND TIGHT
> YOU CAN'T SEE THE
> CELLULITE
> TALL AND SLIM OR SMALL AND GRIM
> OUR TALENT'S GOING TO GLEAM – CUZ ON THIS
> ONE NIGHT A WEEK
> WE CAN DREAM

TINA. From the top!

ALL.

> ONE NIGHT A WEEK
> IT'S TIME TO STEP OUT
> STRIP IT ALL OFF
> AND SHAKE IT ABOUT

ROSE.

> I MAY BE FORTY AND FAT
> DONT GIVE A DAMN ABOUT THAT
> MAYBE LIKE ME YOUR BODY SHIFTS TO PLACES
> THAT DON'T LET YOU REACH YOUR SHOELACES

T, R, D, A, G.	**MX, S, L.**
ONE NIGHT A WEEK	IN THE MIRROR
WE DON'T HAVE A CARE	FIRM AND HARD
'BOUT HOW WE LOOK	FILLING OUT
OR WHAT WE SHOULD WEAR	A LEOTARD
WE'RE ONLY HERE FOR	
A LAUGH	

MRS. FRASER. *(to* **TINA***)*

> THAT'LL BE YOUR EPITAPH

DOT.

> DON'T FORGET SOME OF US
> ARE QUITE ANTIQUE

	MX, S, L.
	'CUZ ON THIS
T, R, D, A, G.	
JUST FOR TONIGHT	ONE NIGHT A WEEK
WE'RE LEAVING OUR CARES	
OUT OF SIGHT	WE CAN DREAM
ON ONE NIGHT A WEEK	

ALL.

> JUST FOR AWHILE
> YOU'LL FIND THERE'S A REASON TO SMILE
> ON ONE NIGHT A WEEK

TINA. Good going you guys, how'd that feel? Okay, let's take one more crack at it and it's five six seven eight...

(As she is saying this, the door is opened and **VIVIENNE** *sticks her head in, unseen by the group. She enters and moves to the front. Although she hasn't been here before, she is undaunted as she waves to catch* **TINA***'s attention.)*

VIVIENNE. Excuse me…excuse me…

(**TINA**'s attention is caught in the mirror. The class stops dancing. **MRS. FRASER** stops playing and they all look at **VIVIENNE**.)

VIVIENNE. Excuse me, is this the tap class?

SHELLEY. No, honey, no – Astro Physics for the Mentally Challenged.

TINA. (moving towards **VIVIENNE**, smiling) Hi, I'm Tina, I teach the class, can I help you?

VIVIENNE. Am I too late to join?

TINA. No of course not – excuse me everyone – just take a sec.

(Having given **VIVIENNE** the once-over, **MRS. FRASER** pointedly holds up the ledger and will pick up a magazine and read it as the others will chat among themselves, some going through steps.)

TINA. Have you done any tap before?

VIVIENNE. (with a careful, precise, rather affected "country club" accent) Well, I did start another class but – well, to be honest, I didn't really like the teacher.

TINA. (smiling) I better not ask who it was then… (She makes to write in the ledger.) Mrs…?

VIVIENNE. Andrews, Mrs. Andrews.

TINA. And what do we call you?

VIVIENNE. Oh – yes. Vivienne.

(As **TINA** completes the ledger entry, **VIVIENNE** takes the opportunity of looking at herself in the mirror, touching her hair, and seeing the others as she does so.)

VIVIENNE. Are there a lot?

TINA. What?

VIVIENNE. I was wondering if you had a lot in the class.

TINA. Not a lot, no: just about the right number.

MRS. FRASER. Like flies. They come out in the summer and die off in the winter. Like flies.

VIVIENNE. When would you like me to pay?

(Still reading, **MRS. FRASER** *holds up the cashbox.)*

MRS. FRASER. *Now.*

*(***VIVIENNE*** takes money from her wallet.* **MAXINE** *meanwhile, is in the process of doing a selling job on* **ANDY**, *holding a blue leotard up against her and guiding her so that they are both looking into the mirror.)*

MAXINE. Oh yeah – that is you, definitely you.

ANDY. You don't think, umm, sleeves, do you?

MAXINE. Not in the blue, no, no can do. I could do sleeves in red, but with your coloring – don't think so.

ANDY. Will you be getting any?

MAXINE. I can never tell. I get what's available, know what I'm saying?

MRS. FRASER. *(not looking up)* I know what you're saying.

ANDY. Umm…could I just *look* at the red?

MAXINE. Look at what you like, darling.

(She digs out a red leotard. **DOROTHY** *tries a step, watched and advised by* **LYNNE** *as* **SHELLEY** *moves to regard herself in the mirror.)*

SHELLEY. Talk about the Goodyear Blimp – you know I can put my bra on backwards and it fits.

ROSE. You've lost weight, Shell.

SHELLEY. Definitely not.

ROSE. Definitely.

SHELLEY. I really pigged out last weekend. Saturday's the big "do" with Eddie's work bunch, and then Sunday his mother's over so I'm out there cookin' up a storm. Oh well, screw it, that's what I say.

VIVIENNE. *(pointing)* Is that where we change?

TINA. Lynne – could you show…

VIVIENNE. No that's all right thank you, I can manage.

(She is about to move away but picks up the empty juice carton and apple core from on top of the piano.)

I'll just get rid of these for you, alrighty?

TINA. Oh…that's very nice of you, Vivienne, thank you.

(VIVIENNE carries the debris into the dressing room as MRS. FRASER glances at TINA (i.e. hello, we've got one of those…) MAXINE is holding a long-sleeved red leotard up against ANDY.)

MAXINE. No, I don't think so…it's the blue, definitely the blue. What do you say, Andy. Ten bucks.

ANDY. Yes, well, okay, fine.

(MAXINE sees GEOFFREY and holds up the red leotard.)

MAXINE. How about a nice leotard, Geoffrey – if you don't want to wear it now, you can always wear it on the beach. *(She nudges ANDY and squeezes the crotch of the leotard.)* Plenty of room for his loose change… *(and she moves away, but remembers and calls back)* How're you fixed for tights?

MRS. FRASER. You're the one should be doing the selling, not her.

TINA. Yes I know all about that, thank you, Glenda.

MRS. FRASER. Turning the place into a Wal-Mart.

(TINA is already moving away, clapping her hands and smiling with)

TINA. Okay. Sorry, people – can't turn down business, right Maxine?

MAXINE. You said it.

TINA. Okay if we can we get you into two lines, please, we're going to look at the step we learned last week… remember…it goes…

(She starts to demonstrate as VIVIENNE comes out of the dressing room, wearing a neat skirt and new tap shoes. There is a hankie up her sleeve.)

VIVIENNE. Sorry to keep you everyone.

TINA. This is Vivienne. Everybody say hi to Vivienne.

(They chorus their hellos as VIVIENNE moves confidently into the front row, admiring herself in the mirror.)

Why don't you stay at the back, Vivienne, so you can watch what we're doing.

(**VIVIENNE** *moves into the back row, unoffended, with a last look and touch of her hair in the mirror as:*)

Don't worry if you get it wrong, you won't get thrown out, it's not an audition – come forward just a natch, Geoffrey – and it's – *(and she demonstrates as)* – three buffaloes to the right and tap step ball change – two cramp rolls brush heel tap heel stamp – and Shelley – you going to be getting some real tap shoes or what?

SHELLEY. Now that I'm such a whiz at it, I guess I'd better.

(**MRS. FRASER** *irritably thumps the keys.*)

TINA. Okay we're going to go through it nice and slow to the music – nice and slow please Glenda and it's five six seven eight…

(**MRS. FRASER** *plays… ONE NIGHT A WEEK…but much too quickly and the dancers stumble and* **TINA** *waves for her to stop.*)

No, that's too fast – take it at…

(She demonstrates the tempo.)

MRS. FRASER. It's exactly the same as last week.

TINA. *(not prepared to argue)* Okay – just a little slower then – and it's five six seven eight…

(**MRS. FRASER** *plays again at exactly the same tempo.*)

Glenda, it's still too fast.

MRS. FRASER. It's exactly the same as last week.

MAXINE. No, it was slower last week – I mean it doesn't bother *me* but…

ROSE. Yes, it was definitely slower, definitely.

DOROTHY. Definitely, yes – wasn't it, Geoffrey?

GEOFFREY. Umm…

TINA. Okay here we go then…five six seven eight…

(**MRS. FRASER** *plays at funereal pace and the dancers stumble.*)

Glenda…it's too slow.

MRS. FRASER. You said it was too fast.

TINA. And now I'm saying it's too slow.

MRS. FRASER. I see. *(She closes the piano lid and stands.)* Fine. When you make up your mind, maybe someone will be kind enough to let me know.

*(Without looking at anyone, she goes into the dressing room. Everyone apart from **VIVIENNE** is used to this performance.)*

TINA. Excuse me… *(She moves to the dressing room.)* Take them through it again, would you, Lynne?

(She goes into the dressing room. There is a moment's silence.)

VIVIENNE. Does she get upset often?

SHELLEY. I think she's goin' through the change of key myself.

LYNNE. Like, which part did she mean?

DOROTHY. I think she meant the last one…that goes…

*(**DOROTHY** slowly demonstrates with her large movements and **LYNNE** joins in, as **ROSE** sits wearily in a chair, adjusting her wig. **GEOFFREY** exits discreetly to the lobby.)*

VIVIENNE. I did consider aerobics.

SHELLEY. Oh I did all that, cantcha tell? My favorite's "The Sponge" – where you lie on the bed all morning *thinking* about going to the gym, but never actually doin' it.

VIVIENNE. There are so many classes nowadays, aren't there? Everyone I know's going to some class or other.

ROSE. That's because we live in a very class-conscious world.

MAXINE. That's a very nice shirt: betcha didn't get it around here.

VIVIENNE. No, Lionel brought it back from Geneva, Switzerland.

SHELLEY. Rosie, you comin' to the Dreamaway for a beer?

ROSE. Are you?

SHELLEY. Where else. Come on – just one. Why not.

(*MAXINE is doing some steps in front of the mirror. VIVIENNE moves to her.*)

VIVIENNE. You're awfully good at it, have you been doing it for long?

MAXINE. It's all in the genes, sweetheart: my mother was frightened by a Busby Berkeley movie.

(*MRS. FRASER comes out of the dressing room and moves straight to the piano, ignoring the others, as though nothing has happened. TINA comes after her.*)

TINA. (*clapping her hands*) Okay sorry, slight misunderstanding, all my fault, let's do it again – everybody ready? (*she suddenly realizes*) Where's Geoffrey?

SHELLEY. (*gesturing towards the lobby restrooms, and adjusting an imaginary fly front*) Target practice…

VIVIENNE. I'll just go get him, alrighty?

(*And before TINA can stop her, VIVIENNE has exited into the lobby where we hear her calling GEOFFREY and knocking on the door to the restroom.*)

TINA. And it's five six seven eight…

(*MRS. FRASER resumes playing – ONE NIGHT A WEEK – and this time to the right tempo, to TINA's obvious relief – and they dance and the lights change.*)

Scene Two

(*The Small Lobby leading into the Gym. One month later.*)

(*7:45 PM*)

(*A main door, right, leading in from outside; a door marked 'RESTROOMS'; and the swinging doors leading through into the Gym. A bench, a water cooler, a fire extinguisher, and a bulletin board copiously covered in various announcements.*)

(It is cold outside and those arriving show signs of it. **GEOFFREY** *sits on a chair, still wearing his overcoat and muffler, coming to the end of a takeout Subway sandwich, holding its wrapper in his other hand. His briefcase is next to him on the bench.)*

(After a moment, **VIVIENNE** *bustles in. She is wearing a leather trenchcoat trimmed in fake fur, and high polished boots. She carries her tote bag and a Hermes shopping bag.)*

(They are somewhat surprised at seeing each other. **GEOFFREY** *gets to his feet, a little awkward at being caught with his sandwich dinner.)*

VIVIENNE. Oh, hi there Geoffey, you're early.

GEOFFREY. Yes, I came right from the office.

VIVIENNE. It's all rush, rush, rush nowadays, isn't it.

GEOFFREY. Usually I have time to go home, but, umm…

(He vaguely indicates the sandwich.)

VIVIENNE. Oh no, go ahead, don't worry about me. Would you like some coffee? I brought some coffee – yes, I'll bet you would.

*(***VIVIENNE*** *takes a thermos from her tote bag, gives* **GEOFFREY** *the cup from the thermos and pours coffee into it. The cup gets very hot and he can just about hold it between his fingers, transferring it from one hand to the other – not that* **VIVIENNE** *notices.)*

VIVIENNE. *(cont.)* I get really thirsty when I'm dancing, don't you? I think all the girls do. Why we can't use the kitchen facilities, I don't know, I mean we're hardly going to mess the place up – not like those cub scouts do. I think I'm going to have a word with the custodian and suggest our own little cupboard or something, with a lock. So you don't work around here, Geoffrey?

GEOFFREY. No, no, downtown.

VIVIENNE. Oh ? What kind of work do you do – if you don't mind me asking?

GEOFFREY. Insurance – car insurance.

VIVIENNE. That must be very interesting – sugar?

*(Before **GEOFFREY** can protest, **VERA** is spooning unwanted sugar into his coffee.)*

Anyway, if you'll excuse me, I just want to have a quick swoosh at the toilet bowl.

*(She produces a toilet brush from her bag and will wave it about, reinforcing her point, sometimes close to **GEOFFREY**'s face.)*

That's why I came early. I mean all kidding aside, it's not very nice in there, is it? I mean there's all kinds of people using it during the week, it's not just us, you have to be so careful. Oh, and I'll just get rid of this for you, alrighty?

*(She relieves him of the sandwich wrapper and goes briskly into the door marked 'RESTROOMS'. **GEOFFREY** watches her go, shaking his head slightly, and drinks some coffee as **ANDY** enters. She wears a dull, shapeless coat over her dance outfit, a hat and little neck scarf, and carries a tote bag. She smiles, a little shy at finding him on his own.)*

ANDY. Hello.

GEOFFREY. *(returning her smile)* Hello.

(a little moment and)

ANDY. Looks like we're the first.

GEOFFREY. No, umm, Vivienne's here. *(He makes a small gesture towards the restrooms.)* She's, umm, on latrine duty.

ANDY. Oh dear.

(Again, that little smile from each of them. We should sense that they really want to communicate.)

Tina's late.

GEOFFREY. Yes, she's usually here by now.

ANDY. No Mrs Fraser either.

GEOFFREY. No. I think Tina usually gives her a lift.

*(**VIVIENNE** comes out of the restroom.)*

VIVIENNE. Geoffrey, would you mind giving me a – oh, hi there Andy, you look nice – sorry, you couldn't give me a hand, could you, I can't get the little doohickey undone.

GEOFFREY. Yes, sure.

(He goes through into the restroom taking his cup.)

VIVIENNE. *(to* **ANDY***)* Sorry to interrupt.

ANDY. You weren't interup –

VIVIENNE. *(calling after* **GEOFFREY***)* Thankyousoverymoocho Geoffrey.

(She smiles at **ANDY***. Confidentially)*

He's very brave, isn't he, Andy? Being the only one with all us girls. I mean he must feel very awkward at times, don't you think?

ANDY. I've never really…

VIVIENNE. I wonder why he comes?

ANDY. Maybe you should ask him.

VIVIENNE. I did. He says he enjoys it.

ANDY. Well then.

VIVIENNE. Yes, I suppose he does. *(even more confidentially)* His wife's dead, you know. Cancer. Forty-two.

ANDY. And his son's in Europe. Yes, I know.

VIVIENNE. Sweden. He's a furniture designer. That must be it then, he enjoys the company. Oh, and I hope you don't mind but I've been meaning to ask you – what's Andy short for?

ANDY. It's not short for anything – it's long for Anne.

*(***GEOFFREY*** *comes out of the restroom.)*

GEOFFREY. All done.

VIVIENNE. Thankyousoverymoocho Geoffrey.

(She briskly relieves him of the cup and busies back into the restroom. **ANDY** *and* **GEOFFREY** *exchange a little smile at her.)*

ANDY. Do you live on West Putnam Street?

GEOFFREY. Emerson. It's just past Putnam.

ANDY. Because I saw you walking there the other night – I think it was Tuesday.

GEOFFREY. I go that way from the station – up over the bridge, and then down to Emerson. It's a little quicker than……

(He vaguely indicates "around the other way." She nods.)

Do you live around…?

ANDY. No. We're over in Parkdale.

(He nods appreciatively. A slight moment and then he takes up his briefcase with:)

GEOFFREY. I guess we'd better, umm…

(He means go into the gym… She nods, smiles. He pushes open the swinging doors and we are into…)

Scene Three

(The YMCA Gym. The same evening.)

(The room is in shadowy darkness except for the frag-mented beams of light thrown in from the streetlights outside.)

(**GEOFFREY** *turns on the overhead lights as he comes in and throughout the following will go around the room switching on electric wall heaters.)*

ANDY. I was going that way to pick up one of my old ladies – I help out at the Senior Center every month – just fetching and carrying really – it's not much but at least it gets them out of the house – some of the older ones are completely alone, you know – it seems so awful, they never speak to a living soul from…

(She realizes she's going on a bit and – as though to make light of it, she sings)

"RIGHT!"

ANDY.

I ALMOST OFFERED YOU A LIFT

GEOFFREY.

OH?

ANDY.

YOU KNOW – I MEAN – THE OTHER NIGHT

GEOFFREY.

AH

ANDY.

I WOULD HAVE STOPPED TO SAY HELLO –

BUT WELL – YOU KNOW – THAT – IT'S NOT…

GEOFFREY.

RIGHT !

ANDY.

I MEAN I REALLY SHOULD HAVE STOPPED

GEOFFREY.

NO

ANDY.

OF COURSE – IT WOULD HAVE BEEN POLITE

GEOFFREY.

ER...

ANDY.

BUT I WAS FEELING SORT OF HURRIED
AND I WORRIED – THAT IS –

GEOFFREY.

RIGHT !

ANDY.

YOU KNOW I REALLY COULD WALK HERE
– IT ISN'T THAT FAR
BUT MY HUSBAND'S INSISTENT
I COME HERE BY CAR
WELL YOU KNOW – LATE AT NIGHT – SO I THOUGHT
THAT YOU MIGHT NEED A RIDE AFTER CLASS –
I MEAN

GEOFFREY.

AH

ANDY

YOU KNOW WHEN THINGS AREN'T GOING WELL?

GEOFFREY.

MMM...

ANDY.

WHEN LIFE HAS DEALT A HEAVY BLOW

GEOFFREY.

YES

ANDY.

YOU FIND IT EASIER TO BEAR IT – IF YOU SHARE IT
THAT IS –

GEOFFREY.

OH

ANDY

SHOULDN'T PEOPLE SHARE THEIR TROUBLES?

GEOFFREY.

MORE OR LESS – THAT IS YES
AND – ER – NO

ANDY.

> NO ONE HAS TO BE LONELY
> FRIENDS ARE SUCH A DELIGHT
> AND I KNOW BEING LONELY
> IS A TERRIBLE PLIGHT
>
> SO I THOUGHT I SHOULD ASK – THAT IS,
> YOU MIGHT CARE TO – HAVE A TALK
> IF YOU LIKE – MAYBE –

GEOFFREY.

> RIGHT!

ANDY.

> I MEAN IF YOU SHOULD NEED A FRIEND

GEOFFREY.

> YES

ANDY.

> YOU NEVER KNOW WHAT MAY OCCUR

GEOFFREY.

> NO

ANDY.

> NOW THERE'S A SYMPATHETIC EAR THAT
> YOU'LL FIND HERE THAT – YOU KNOW

GEOFFREY.

> ER…

ANDY.

> IF YOU NEED SOMEONE TO TALK TO
> AND ONE DAY – WHO CAN SAY
> YOU JUST MIGHT
> TELL ME THEN – I MEAN WHEN
> IT FEELS

BOTH.

> RIGHT!

> (**ROSE** *and* **SHELLEY** *come in noisily.* **SHELLEY** *wears a short down parka over her dance gear and is chewing gum.* **ROSE** *wears a neat dufflecoat and headscarf. Each carries a bag with shoes etc.*)

ROSE. Nine-thirty he finally comes home –

ROSE/SHELL. Hi Andy, Hey Geoffrey…

ROSE. – "And where've *you* been?" I say. "We'll discuss that later" he says, "but in the meantime, dearly beloved, where's my dinner?"

SHELLEY. Whatcha do – throw it at him?

ROSE. It was already in the garbage, so I threw the bag at him.

(She giggles and continues straight across towards the dressing room.)

Blessed Jesus! The look on that man's face. *(pseudo-thunderous)* Next time, I'll kill him.

(And she goes into the dressing room. **SHELLEY** *moves straight downstage to regard herself unlovingly in the mirror.* **GEOFFREY** *sits at his usual place, in front of the stage.* **ANDY** *sits near the piano.)*

SHELLEY. Don't you believe a word of it, she's nuts about him. They're crazy about each other. He's kinda dishy too, for his age. He's got this phenomenal bone structure and beautiful nails. Unlike *my* husband. I swear, Eddie's got hands like the soles of your feet. He used to be a scaffold-worker. Good thing, eh Geoffrey?

(pseudo-ruefully looking at her body)

Climbing up this baby's no picnic, lemme tell you.

(She moves to the electric heater near the piano, raises her coat and warms her generous behind.)

We met 'em for a beer one night. So cute – they were holding hands, looking into each other's eyes, whispering sweet doo-dahs – he even holds the door open for her.

ANDY. That must be very…nice.

SHELLEY. Twenty years they been hitched, and three kids – it's more like a freakin' miracle. Mind you, they're very religious. I wonder if that's got anything to do with it.

ANDY. I don't know. I don't think so. I'd like to think so but…

SHELLEY. I'm a Catholic, you know. Well. Vaguely. Some great great grandfather came over from Ireland all gung ho until he found out the Catholic church was gonna charge two dollars to be buried in their cemetary – so he said screw this and became a Methodist. No, I reckon it's just luck of the draw. Sometimes I look at Eddie and think what are you doing with this person but then I think to myself, Shelley hon, bearing in mind the gaping holes in your own personality, you are a very lucky girl. I gotta pee before I explode.

(She moves towards the swinging doors as **MAXINE** *comes in.* **MAXINE** *is wearing a smart coat over her dance gear, and carries a bag with two new shirts in it.)*

MAXINE. Good evening to Shelley, how's Shelley, hello Andy, how's Andy, hello Geoffrey, how's Geoffrey?

SHELLEY. *(over her shoulder at the doors)* Hello Maxine – had a good week, did you?

(She gives a big wink to **ANDY** *and goes out.* **MAXINE** *slumps into a chair, stretching out her legs. During the following,* **GEOFFREY** *will be changing into his tap shoes.)*

MAXINE. What a day, I'm lucky to be alive. Don't ask, you do not want to know. The whole day I'm on red alert. I really didn't think I was going to make it tonight, every time I open the door the phone rings. Is it for me? Forget it. I'm just the answering service. It's for Wonderboy: Prince Charmless. I should have his social life. What do they see in him? Anyway. I'm here thank God and that's all I care about. So. How are ya?

ANDY. Fine.

MAXINE. Can I be honest? You don't look fine. You look like you could use a break.

ANDY. Why do you say things like that?

*(***DOROTHY** *comes in. She wears oversized boots, thick pants, a parka, a vest with reflector tape, a head lamp, and carries a knapsack containing her purse, bike pump, and dance gear.)*

DOROTHY. Hi everyone.

MAXINE. Hello Dorothy, how's Dorothy?

(**DOROTHY** *goes straight through into the dressing room.*)

Yeah I know, I'm terrible, I should mind my own business. But do yourself a favor, get him to take you away for a couple of days, it works wonders, believe me.

ANDY. (*stiffly, aware of* **GEOFFREY**) Yes, well, I'm afraid that isn't possible at the moment. And as you say, maybe you should mind your own business.

(*She takes her bag through into the dressing room.* **MAXINE** *sees* **GEOFFREY** *looking at her.*)

MAXINE. If you want something, it's possible, believe me, it's possible.

(**GEOFFREY** *will take off his overcoat and sports jacket to reveal a bright handknit multi-coloured sweater vest.* **VIVIENNE** *bustles in with her bag, now wearing yellow rubber gloves and holding a can of air freshener…followed by* **SHELLEY**.)

VIVIENNE. Hello Maxine, don't you look nice. Darling coat.

(*And with a discreet squirt of the spray,* **VIVIENNE** *goes into the dressing room.*)

SHELLEY. She's at it again.

(*She puts a fresh stick of gum in her mouth and sits on the floor to put on a pair of new bright red tap shoes as:*)

MAXINE. What is it this time?

SHELLEY. Now she's stuck up a whole list of instructions on how to use the john.

MAXINE. Like your shoes, Shell.

(**ROSE**, *now wearing her dance gear, and usual beads – including a large crucifix around her neck – comes out of the dressing room, giggling to herself.*)

SHELLEY. So what are we so cheerful about?

ROSE. Nothing, nothing…

MAXINE. Vivienne's just given her nine out of ten for toilet training.

ROSE. Do you ever make love first thing in the morning?

SHELLEY. Gimme a break. He can't even raise an eyebrow until he's spent six years in the bathroom. What do they *do* in there for so long anyway?

(**ANDY** *comes out of the dressing room with her bag. She wears the new leotard, still has the small scarf around her neck, and is a little self-conscious.*)

MAXINE. Nice, very becoming.

SHELLEY. Pretty, Andy.

ROSE. Yeah.

MAXINE. That reminds me, Geoffrey – those shirts I promised you.

(*As* **DOROTHY** *comes out of the dressing room with her bag,* **MAXINE** *takes some packaged shirts from her bag and tosses them to* **GEOFFREY**.)

DOROTHY. Anyone know what's happening?

ANDY. It's almost eight o'clock – do you think Tina's coming or what?

MAXINE. Yeah, where is she?

SHELLEY. She has to be comin'.

ANDY. Well something could have happened.

DOROTHY. Happened – yes.

SHELLEY. *(of her body)* Don't tell me I lugged this load over here for nothin'.

ROSE. Don't worry, ladies – if worse comes to worse, I can teach the class.

(*She demonstrates her dancing ability.*)

I got three speeds: Start, Stumble, and Fall.

SHELLEY. Careful, you'll knock your wig off.

MAXINE. Is it growing out yet, Rose?

ROSE. He tells me it's like sleeping with a buncha Brillo pads.

SHELLEY. Aw, in three months it'll be all gorgeous and curly again, watch.

ROSE. But that's the whole point: I wanted it all gorgeous and straight.

(She adjusts her wig in the mirror as:)

MAXINE. You should always read the directions on the box.

SHELLEY. Better yet, you should always try it out on the dog.

ROSE. Jesus don't preach! I got enough trouble. *(She does a few steps.)* Look at me – if the damn wig isn't falling off I'm knocking myself out with the crucifix.

(VIVIENNE comes out of the dressing room and moves directly to SHELLEY. She wears leotard, legwarmers and carries a small Zip-loc bag full of coasters, and a waste-basket.)

VIVIENNE. Excuse me…I hope you don't mind me asking, but do you chew gum because you've given up smoking?

SHELLEY. No – because I might meet someone nice.

VIVIENNE. It's just that I keep finding it everywhere.

SHELLEY. That's because I keep puttin' it everywhere. *(She drops the gum noisily into the empty wastebasket.)* I could sure use someone like you at home, Vivienne.

(VIVIENNE will put the wastebasket down, open her Zip-loc and buzz around distributing coasters underneath any cans or bottles on piano, windowledges etc. as)

ANDY. Is Lynne here? She could start the class, couldn't she? She knows all the steps.

DOROTHY. She won't be here for half an hour.

ROSE. That's right, she's working.

DOROTHY. Working – yes.

ANDY. Well, I think we ought to do something, don't you?

VIVIENNE. Have we got a problem?

DOROTHY. Tina's not here.

GEOFFREY. Can I make a suggestion?

ROSE. Geoffrey is about to make a suggestion.

MAXINE. Hey. Geoffery – I hope your sex life is as busy as that sweater.

(ANDY moves to one side, irritation growing.)

ROSE. Now then, ladies, let the man speak.

SHELLEY. Order!

VIVIENNE. Yes, come on Geoffrey, what were you going to say?

GEOFFREY. All I was going to say was…why don't we start the warm-up while we're waiting? That's all.

SHELLEY. That is brilliant. Brilliant.

ROSE. All those in favor of starting the warm-up?

(Various hands go up.)

ROSE. All those against?

ANDY. *(a sudden flash of irritation)* Oh come on this is ridiculous!

(They all turn to look at her.)

I'm sorry but it's just…it's just ridiculous. We're not children.

(a moment)

DOROTHY. Well, we'd better do something, I s'pose.

MAXINE. Can anyone play the piano?

ROSE. Who needs the piano? *(Cod-Jamaican)* Just follow me, girls, I got music in ma soul.

(She moves to the mirror and begins her uncoordinated version of the warm-up routine.)

SHELLEY *(teasingly)* I thought you people could move…

ROSE. Sure we can move. Problem is, in my case, it all moves in different directions.

"DON'T ASK ME"

ROSE.

I GOT MUSIC IN MY SOUL
FEEL LIKE DANCIN' DOWN THE STREET
– TROUBLE IS MY SOUL AIN'T BEEN
CONNECTED TO MY FEET
SO IF YOU WANT SOMEONE TO SHOW YOU
HOW TO SET YOUR BODY FREE
– DON'T ASK ME

STILL THAT MUSIC'S IN MY SOUL
AND THAT SONG IS IN MY HEAD
AND THAT'S THE WAY I KNOW BABE
I'M NOT READY TO BE DEAD
SO IF YOU HAVE TO FIND A REASON
TO ENJOY THAT MELODY
– DON'T ASK ME

GOD GAVE US THE FACILITY
TO JUMP RIGHT OUT OF THE GROOVE
WE ALL GOT THAT ABILITY
SO PROVE IT – MOVE IT

WITH THAT MUSIC IN YOUR SOUL
THERE'S A SONG YOU GOTTA SING
SING THAT SONG TOGETHER –
GONNA MAKE THOSE RAFTERS RING
AND IF YOU WANT SOMEONE TO LEAD YOU
IN THREE PART HARMONY –
DON'T ASK ME – NO DON'T ASK ME

EVERYONE GOT A RHYTHM THEY CAN TAP TO

ALL.

CLAP TO

ROSE.

EVERYONE KNOWS SOME MUSIC THEY CAN SING TO

ALL.

SWING TO

ROSE.

EVERYONE GOT A TUNE THAT MAKES YOU FEEL GOOD

ALL.

REAL GOOD

ROSE.

IF YOU JUST LET YOURSELF GET CARRIED AWAY

(dance break)

SO IF YOU WANT SOMEONE TO SHOW YOU
HOW TO SET YOUR BODY FREE
DON'T ASK ME
NO, DON'T ASK ME

WITH THAT MUSIC IN YOUR SOUL
THERE'S A SONG YOU GOTTA SING
SING THAT SONG TOGETHER
GONNA MAKE THOSE RAFTERS RING
BUT WHEN YOU WANT SOMEONE TO FINISH
THIS ENDLESS RHAPSODY – DON'T ASK ME
ASK THE MOON – ASK THE SUN
GO ASK ANYONE
BUT DON'T ASK ME

GEOFFREY. One mo' time!

*(Totally caught up in the spirit of things, **GEOFFREY** moves quickly to sit at the piano and starts to play a more-than-adequate rendition of Rose's song – much to the surprise and delight of the others – so that they are singing and clapping along as)*

*(**TINA** and **MRS. FRASER** enter. **TINA** carries her tap shoes and bag, **MRS. FRASER** her music case and bag.)*

*(The class, each in turn, see **TINA** and **MRS. FRASER** and stop dancing, unbeknownst to **GEOFFREY** who is lost in the music and continues playing and singing:)*

"Don't ask me…no don't ask me…."

*(**MRS. FRASER** moves straight across to glare down at him. **GEOFFREY** suddenly realizes she's there and jerks away from the piano. **TINA**, amused, will sit near the piano, pulling on her tap shoes as **MRS. FRASER** sits at the piano, taking out a tissue to flick at the keys.)*

TINA. Really really sorry everyone – traffic. We'll do the full hour, I swear. Anyway – *(she smiles at them)* – I see you haven't been wasting your time.

SHELLEY. You know us, Tina, passionate.

MAXINE. We thought you'd deserted us.

TINA. Now would I do a thing like that?

VIVIENNE. *(hand up, moving forward)* Would you like me to go collect everyone's class money, Tina?

TINA. Oh, we can do that later.

MRS. FRASER. Just as long as we remember…

GEOFFREY. *(handing her the key)* The key, umm, Tina, for the umm, gym.

TINA. Thanks, Geoffrey, great.

> *(***LYNNE** *hurries in, wearing her nurse's uniform and carrying her bag.)*

LYNNE. Sorry, you guys.

> *(She sits and quickly unlaces her work shoes as the others ad lib their "Hello, Lynnes".)*

TINA. Okay – so what d'you say we get right into the piece we started last week.

SHELLEY. Goody! What piece we started last week?

DOROTHY. You remember…it goes…

> *(She demonstrates with her usual extravagance.)*

TINA. Thank you, Dorothy, on second thought maybe we better go from the top of the routine and it's five six seven eight…

> *(***MRS. FRASER** *begins to play a version of "ONE NIGHT A WEEK" and they dance…with* **TINA** *calling out the steps.…)*

> *(The lights change.)*

> *(***VIVIENNE** *taps her way across and presents* **MRS. FRASER** *with an apple and taps her way back to join the others.)*

Scene Four

(Later the same evening.)

(The Lobby, with Dorothy's bicycle in it. Empty for a moment and then **DOROTHY** *and* **LYNNE** *come through from the Gym.* **DOROTHY***, who is wearing her helmet, unlocks her bike.)*

DOROTHY. I hate talking about him like this, but I mean, he *is* my brother. What I mean is, I mean, she is his mother as well as mine, you'd think he'd want to help out, wouldn't you? I mean it's not her fault she's an invalid, is it?

LYNNE. No, of course it isn't.

DOROTHY. Isn't – no. And when you think of all she's done for him – well, both of us.

LYNNE. I'm afraid people can be...

DOROTHY. Very selfish – yes. And he can be so, well, insensitive. It's all right for you, he says, you're not married. I know I'm not married but I'm entitled to some sort of life, aren't I? I mean, one night a week I have, to get away, and even then he doesn't offer to help. I have to pay a sitter. I don't know – it's so unfair.

LYNNE. The thing is – the thing is not to think about *him* but to, you know, like, think about your mother – to think about, like you said, everything she's done for you. What I mean is – it's looking for, like, the good things instead of the bad...

DOROTHY. ...the bad – yes – yes, you're right, Lynne, of course you are. I'm just feeling sorry for myself and I have to stop it... *(she gives herself a little slap on the arm and)* ...stop it, Dorothy.

   (ROSE, SHELLEY *and* **MAXINE** *come noisily out of the Gym.)*

ROSE. You girls joining us for a little... *(She mimes drinking.)*

LYNNE. I wish. Got to go study. Sorry.

SHELLEY. Aw, one quick drink won't hurt. Come on. Tina's comin'.

*(***DOROTHY*** *and* **LYNNE** *ad lib their "no, reallys".)*

MAXINE. Well we're at the Dreamaway if you change your mind – come on, goils.

(They exit, noisily, with:)

ROSE. Just one, and then it's home to Big Daddy.

SHELLEY. No no, make him wait, Rosie – get him all excited…

*(***DOROTHY*** *and* **LYNNE** *watch them go. Then* **LYNNE** *gives* **DOROTHY** *a little smile (i.e. "those girls")…and)*

LYNNE. Do you ever like…do you ever wish *you* were married?

DOROTHY. I don't really think about it. No, I mean, you know. Sort of. You know. There is this – man – in the office but…you know. One day maybe. When my mother…you know. Do *you?*

LYNNE. Oh no…not *married*…I mean, not yet…I've had boyfriends, yeah, sure….well, *a* boy…but anyway I want to – you know, like get my degree and everything first. You know. My work.

"LOVE TO"

LYNNE.
I WOULD LOVE TO
CHANGE MY OUTLOOK

DOROTHY.
[LOOK – YES]

LYNNE.
LOOK MY LIFESTYLE NEEDS AN OVERHAUL
WOULD YOU LIKE TO

DOROTHY.
[LIKE TO CHANGE]

LYNNE.
CHANGE YOUR LIFESTYLE?

DOROTHY.
[HAIRSTYLE – YES]

BOTH.

    BUY A REALLY PRETTY –

DOROTHY.

    COVERALL

LYNNE. Dress

    I'D LOVE TO CHANGE

    BUT I'M SCARED

    AND MAYBE IT'S TOO SOON

DOROTHY.

    OR MAYBE IT'S TOO LATE

BOTH.

    PERHAPS I SHOULDN'T WAIT

DOROTHY.

    I WOULD LOVE TO

LYNNE.

    LOVE TO CHANGE

DOROTHY.

    CHANGE

BOTH.

    MY OUTLOOK

LYNNE.

    MY ZIPCODE

DOROTHY.

    MY LAST NAME

BOTH.

    AND GIVE MY LIFE A SHOVE

    TO MEET THE MAN I'D LOVE

DOROTHY.

    LOVE

BOTH.

    TO LOVE

    SOMEONE DIFFERENT

    SOMEONE SPECIAL

    AND IF THERE'S AN ANGEL

    WHO'S LISTENING UP ABOVE

    I HAVE IN MIND A MAN

THE VERY KIND OF MAN
I'D LOVE

DOROTHY.
LOVE TO

LYNNE.
TO LOVE

DOROTHY.
LOVE TO

BOTH.
LOVE

(A moment, each of them with her own private dream. Then **DOROTHY** *suddenly makes up her mind, pushing her bike towards the outer door which* **LYNNE** *moves to hold open for her as:)*

DOROTHY. I think I will go for a drink after all. Yes – this is my night out. See you next week, Lynne…

*(***DOROTHY** *exits. A moment and)*

LYNNE. Yeah. See you next week.

(She stands for a moment and suddenly looks and feels very much alone. But she does a little time step to raise her spirits and exits cheerily.)

(The lights change and we are into…)

Scene Five

*(The Dreamaway, a popular local bar/hangout, mini-
mally represented.* TINA, MAXINE, SHELLEY, *and* ROSE
*sit at a table. Each has a near-empty glass of wine or
beer. They are probing* TINA *about her showbiz background and are fascinated.)*

SHELLEY. Did you always wanna be a dancer?

TINA. Did I always want to be a dancer. Yes. Yes, I suppose
I always did.

ROSE. You must have been really something.

TINA. Not bad.

MAXINE. D'you miss it?

TINA. *(smiling)* You mean, why'd I give it up? There wasn't
any work. Not for me there wasn't, anyway. It's an over-
crowded profession, the union's hopeless and chorus
girls of a "certain age" aren't too high on the grocery
list.

*(*DOROTHY *enters with a tray bearing three wines and
a beer for the others and an orange juice for herself. She
will distribute the drinks and sit on a bar stool, opening her small bottle of Tropicana and pouring it into an
empty glass.)*

Hey, don't get me wrong, I love teaching, I get a real
buzz from it, I mean it, and you girls are great, really
great, I really look forward to these classes.

MAXINE. Did you do any big Broadway shows?

TINA. A few. In the chorus. I understudied the lead a couple
of times but never went on – almost, but – nope, not
quite. It's the morning you wake up and realize you
have no more expectations. That's when you make the
big decision. So…I made it. *(She smiles, finishes her wine
and)* Gotta go – Listen, thanks for the wine – see you
next week.

*(She gathers up her bag and quickly goes as they ad lib
their goodnights and watch her go.)*

MAXINE. There goes a lady who's always on the run.

DOROTHY. Run – yes.

SHELLEY. Yeah well, keeps your weight down, I suppose.

MAXINE. I think she's got money problems. Ever notice her shoes? She always wears the same shoes.

SHELLEY. She's not makin' a whole lot out of us, that's for sure – not after she's paid for the gym.

ROSE. And Mrs. Fraser.

MAXINE. Even seven nights a week she ain't gonna make a fortune.

SHELLEY. What about her guy?

MAXINE. What *about* her guy?

*(**SHELLEY** and **ROSE** chorus a "yeah"…and after a moment, **DOROTHY** chips in with a "yes" too. They drink. Each with their own thoughts.)*

MAXINE. Your son got himself a job yet, Rose?

ROSE. Everywhere he tries, it's the same story.

SHELLEY. I think it's lousy for kids nowadays.

DOROTHY. Nowadays – yes.

ROSE. The whole time he was at school, we kept telling him: no diploma, no work. And the way he talks to his father – we didn't bring up our children to talk like that.

MAXINE. They're all the same. Look at Little Lord LameBrain: one minute he's in a rock band, next minute he's in a coma. Know what the latest is? He's decided he wants to go to art school. Art school? He can't even draw a deep breath without fainting.

*(**SHELLEY** flutters fingers towards an unseen someone.)*

ROSE. Stop – flirting.

SHELLEY. I'm not flirting, I'm deadly serious. Least *he* thinks I am. *(And she gives another little wave and holds her come-on smile.)* Ahh…aren't they pathetic, men? All you gotta do is give'em a little pat on the head and they wag their tail like a stupid cocker spaniel. Look at him, he really thinks he's gonna score…Sad, isn'it?

"WHAT DO MEN THINK?"

SHELLEY.

LOOK AT HIM – HE'S OK
IN A SMALL BALDING FAT KINDA WAY

MAXINE.

AND HIS FRIEND WITH THE MUTT
I MEAN– EVEN THE DOG'S GOT A GUT

SHELLEY.

I JUST FLASHED THEM MY LOOK
NOW THEY THINK THAT I'VE SWALLOWED THE HOOK

MAXINE.

WIND 'EM UP – WATCH 'EM GO

BOTH.

IT'S THE GREATEST ENJOYMENT I KNOW

DO MEN THINK A LITTLE FLIRT
MEANS "HORMONES ON RED ALERT"
YES, THEY DO – SEE HIM WINK
ASK ME NOT – WHAT DO MEN THINK?

SHELLEY. There's that Vernon guy.

MAXINE. Who's Vernon?

SHELLEY. This amazingly dubious person I met here last week.

ROSE. Honey, you gotta stop talking to these bozos.

SHELLEY. Get off it, Rose, you give me an earache.

DOROTHY. Earache – yes.

SHELLEY.

SEE THAT GEEK ON HIS OWN
LOOK THE ONE MAKIN' LOVE TO HIS PHONE
HE'S BEEN GLUED TO MY BUST
SINCE I GAVE IT A BIT OF A THRUST

MAXINE. He should be so lucky.

SHELLEY.

LOOK HE THINKS HE'S ALL SET
WHAT A BIG DISAPPOINTMENT HE'LL GET

ROSE (*joins*)

> AREN'T THEY SWEET? AREN'T THEY SAD?

MAX(*joins*)

> THEY DON'T KNOW THEY'RE THE ONES
> WHO'VE BEEN HAD

ALL.

> DO MEN THINK WE'RE BIG ON SEX
> WITH GUYS WITH SMALL INTELLECTS
> THAT ONE'S GOT A MISSING LINK
> HE CAN ROT – WHAT DO MEN THINK?

DOROTHY. Doesn't your husband mind?

SHELLEY. What, that I'm having a night out?

DOROTHY. Out – yes.

SHELLEY. Well, Thursday's my night out. Very simple. He babysits, I go out.

ROSE. He'd mind if he thought you were batting your eyes at Ben & Jerry over there.

SHELLEY. Oh, he *knows.*

DOROTHY. No way – you mean you – you – talk to him about it?

SHELLEY. (*winking at* **MAXINE**) But of course, Dorothy. He loves it. That's why I do it. Mind you, if he believed me he'd kill me. What he enjoys is the *idea* of bein' jealous – and it does wonders for your sex life which, let's face it, takes a severe beating after the first few months of hangin' from the chandelier.

DOROTHY. Chandelier – yes…Pardon?

MAXINE.

> SINCE THE WORLD FIRST BEGAN
> THERE'S BEEN NOTHING SO DUMB AS A MAN

SHELLEY.

> THEY AINT GOT MUCH UP THERE
> CUZ THEIR BRAINS ARE IN THEIR UNDERWEAR

ALL. (*this couplet sung in thick Brooklynese:*)

> DO MEN THINK A SINGLE THOUGHT
> THAT'S NOT SEX OR BEER OR SPORT

ALL. *(cont.)*

> NO THEY DON'T AND AREN'T WE GLAD?
> AREN'T THEY SWEET - AREN'T THEY SAD?
> SO WHEN THEY BUY YOU A DRINK
> JUST DON'T ASK WHAT DO MEN THINK?

> *(In turn,* **SHELLEY** *and* **ROSE** *and* **MAXINE** *each flutter fingers towards an unseen someone as each in turn discreetly exits…* **MAXINE**, *the last to go, pausing behind the unwitting* **DOROTHY** *to mime to the unseen someone that he'll be A-OK with* **DOROTHY**…*so that now only* **DOROTHY** *is left – and she, caught up in the naughtiness of it all, flutters fingers towards an unseen someone and turns to the girls so that they may collude in her naughtiness…)*

DOROTHY. I did it…

> *(For the first time,* **DOROTHY** *realizes she's alone. As she gulps down her juice and exits quickly – we hear the sound of* **MRS. FRASER** *at the piano and the lights change and we are into…)*

Scene Six

(The YMCA Gym. A month later.)

(The class, led by a smiling **TINA***, is coming to the end of a session, danced to ONE NIGHT A WEEK. The session has been a good one and they are all enjoying it.)*

TINA. Way to go, you guys – that was really good, didn't you think? Whoo!

(She is patting her chest and sounding more breathless than she perhaps really is. Several of the class are genuinely breathless but all are very pleased with themselves, some whooping with pleasure as:)

Just a couple of notes. Rose – you're still not getting the scissors. It's… *(She demonstrates.)* …Yeah?

ROSE. The thing is, I don't really see myself as a scissors person.

TINA. Well, keep trying, you never know. Lynne – it's… *(She demonstrates.)* …Yeah?

LYNNE. *(repeating the step)* Oh right, I was forgetting the…. *(She does the step she was missing out.)*

TINA. There you go.

DOROTHY. *(putting up her hand)* Was I all right in the middle part, Tina?

TINA. Much better – but it still needs to be just that teeny bit smaller – *(She demonstrates.)* – not so much work – nice and relaxed, yeah?

DOROTHY. Relaxed – yes.

TINA. And Shelley – *(She demonstrates.)* – you're still starting off on the same foot.

SHELLEY. Yeah, I know it's chronic.

TINA. Any idea what the problem is?

SHELLEY. No – I just seem to use whatever foot comes to hand.

TINA. Any other problems? Maxine? Anyone? No? Okay, that's it for tonight then, we'll pick it up from there next week – and once again good work everyone, you can be really pleased with yourselves. Thank you.

(Immediately, **MRS. FRASER** *plays a piano roll as the class applauds* **TINA** *as is the custom at the end of a session.* **MRS. FRASER** *immediately starts putting her music away as* **MAXINE** *does a flashy little step.)*

MAXINE. Look Ma, I'm dancing!

SHELLEY Michael Flatley, eat your heart out.

(She does a little clod-hopping routine and she and **MAXINE** *finish together with the stamp-stamp hands out position of "how's that?"* **DOROTHY** *and* **LYNNE** *practice a step, mainly for Dorothy's benefit…as the others change and* **VIVIENNE** *bustles around, humming the tune they've just danced to, putting various debris including two cartons of orange juice, a Coke can, and a banana skin from the piano – into the wastebasket.* **TINA** *– all part of the routine by now – waylays her and, with a glance in* **MRS. FRASER**'s *direction, removes her cigarettes from the wastebasket…as* **MRS. FRASER** *collects her things and reads her magazine.)*

*(***ANDY** *moves to* **GEOFFREY**, *collecting signatures for a petition.)*

*(***TINA** *heads for the door with her cigarettes and lighter.)*

VIVIENNE. I hope you don't mind me asking, Tina, but have you ever tried to stop smoking?

TINA. Yes, I did once but I got really cranky and I ate too much and I put on weight and I had to buy new clothes and I upset my fella and I've got enough hassles without all that – so – I smoke.

(She smiles at **VIVIENNE** *and heads through the swinging doors.* **VIVIENNE** *makes to move away but sees a sock hanging over the back of a chair and takes it up between finger and thumb and continues into the dressing room as* **ANDY** *moves to* **LYNNE** *and* **DOROTHY** *for*

more signatures and **ROSE** *heads for the swinging doors.*
SHELLEY *moves close to the mirror to apply lipstick.*)

ANDY. *(generally)* Would anybody else like to sign the petition?

ROSE. What petition?

ANDY. About the cell tower being built over at Meadowbrook.

MAXINE. Andy's very active in these matters.

ANDY. Well, yes, I do think it's necessary to…

MAXINE. She's on the protest committee.

SHELLEY. OK, Andygirl, lemme see it.

(She signs the petition as **LYNNE** *and* **DOROTHY** *go into the dressing room, passing* **VIVIENNE** *who is coming out.)*

VIVIENNE. Has anyone seen a little gold belt?

MAXINE. *(holding up a belt from a chair)* Is this it?

VIVIENNE. Oh there it is, thankyousoverymoocho, Maxine.

ANDY. If anyone's interested, there's a meeting at the town hall this Saturday.

VIVIENNE. I'm going to a wedding this Saturday.

MAXINE. Anyone you know?

VIVIENNE. Lionel's cousin. It's going to be very grand – they're putting up a tent in the back yard. I like weddings, don't you?

SHELLEY. Not a lot.

VIVIENNE. Mine was lovely if I do say so myself.

SHELLEY. Mine was quite boring actually, I'm sorry I went.

VIVIENNE. I can remember every detail of mine.

SHELLEY. So can I.

VIVIENNE. Can you, Maxine?

MAXINE. When it comes to my weddings, instant recoil, darling, instant recoil.

VIVIENNE. Have you been married a lot?

MAXINE. Only the two times, Vivienne, don't get excited.

VIVIENNE. I didn't know you'd been married before, Maxine.

SHELLEY. You sure do like to keep on top a things, don'tcha Vivienne?

VIVIENNE. No, I'm just saying.

MAXINE. From now on I'll send you my press releases. *(to* ANDY, *of the petition)* Let me see that, sweetie.

VIVIENNE. Of course, the thing about divorce, it's the children that really suffer, isn't it?

MAXINE. What did I need kids for, I had him.

SHELLEY. One of those, was he?

MAXINE. What really clinched it for me was the day I came home and found him admiring this set of love bites on his neck. Another woman I might have dealt with but these were self-inflicted.

VIVIENNE. But you're happy now, aren't you, Maxine? You don't mind me asking, do you?

MAXINE. Happy, what's happy? You pretend to be happy, sometimes you end up happy. I'd be a lot happier if someone could tell me how to bring up step-children.

(TINA comes in through the swinging doors, followed by ROSE. VIVIENNE will go into the dressing room. TINA automatically sets her cigarettes and lighter on top of the piano.)

TINA. Okay. Is there anyone who hasn't paid yet?

MRS. FRASER. *(without looking up from her reading and automatically depositing* TINA*'s cigarettes in the wastebasket)* Shelley.

SHELLEY. Oh sorry, Miss Tina, sorry, right away – quick, Rose, lend me five, wouldja?

(She will borrow the money from ROSE *and take it to* TINA *during)*

MAXINE. *(gelling her hair into position in the mirror)* So who's up for The Dreamaway tonight?

SHELLEY. Me! Me! Me! How 'bout you, Tina – wanna come wet your whistle?

TINA. Not tonight thanks – got to get back.

*(She will collect her things and, shooting a look of controlled irritation at **MRS. FRASER**, retrieve her cigarettes yet again as)*

SHELLEY. Keeps you on a tight leash, yeah?

MRS. FRASER. *(to herself but loud and clear)* He's never there.

MAXINE. I am in dire need of alcohol tonight. Mr. Amazing Lazy Bum's got the house full of the usual Beastie Boys. God alone knows what's happening to my Naugahyde. Yeah, why not – let his father deal with him for a change.

ROSE. Mister Geoffrey?

GEOFFREY. No, I've got some work to catch up on.

SHELLEY. Oh come on, Geoffsy – come help us spend your hard earned salary.

GEOFFREY. No, not this week, really.

MRS. FRASER. Don't anyone ask me.

MAXINE. How about you, Mrs. Fraser?

MRS. FRASER. I don't go to nightclubs, thankyouverymuch.

ROSE. Come on, Mrs. F, we'll kick back and relax.

SHELLEY. Anyway, it's not a nightclub, it's just a dumb bar.

MRS. FRASER. I don't drink.

SHELLEY. You gotta drink, Mrs. Fraser, otherwise your liver gets all bunged up.

MRS. FRASER. I'm referring to liquor.

MAXINE. Is that because you're a vegetarian?

MRS. FRASER. That certainly enters into it, yes.

SHELLEY. Well, we can have a drink and you can chew on a carrot.

*(**VIVIENNE** comes out of the dressing room, immaculately dressed, ready to leave.)*

VIVIENNE. I haven't done the coasters, Tina!

SHELLEY. Oh my gawd…

SHELLEY/ROSE/MAXINE. Vivienne hasn't done the coasters, Tina!

TINA. Don't worry, Vivienne, I'll get 'em.

VIVIENNE. We're not the only ones who use this place, you know.

MAXINE. I hope not – there's a jockstrap hanging up out there.

(**DOROTHY** and **LYNNE** come out of the dressing room. **DOROTHY** with her crash helmet on, etc. They call their goodnights as they go out. **ANDY** takes her petition to **TINA**.)

ANDY. Would you mind, Tina?

TINA. No of course. Glad to.

(She signs the petition as **GEOFFREY** takes the opportunity of making a discreet exit, calling out his goodnights. They ad lib their goodnights to him…**ANDY**'s noticeably louder than the others. She offers the petition to **MRS. FRASER**.)

ANDY. Mrs. Fraser?

MRS. FRASER. I don't sign petitions, thank you.

(**VIVIENNE** moves to check her hair and makeup in the mirror. Behind her, **MAXINE** nudges **ROSE**.)

MAXINE. (somewhat unwillingly) Vivienne, you coming for a drink?

VIVIENNE. No I don't think so, thank you, I'm not dressed or anything.

SHELLEY. It's only a dumb bar.

VIVIENNE. Yes I know, but I couldn't, not like this.

SHELLEY. Like what?

VIVIENNE. My hair and everything. Besides, I'm all sweaty.

SHELLEY. Well I'm not sweaty.

VIVIENNE. It may be February outside, but it's always August under your armpits.

SHELLEY. Eeeyoo – very nice. I'll remember that…

VIVIENNE. I mean, all kidding aside, but it's true, isn't it? Besides, Lionel might be phoning from Stuttgart, Germany. Bye Tina, see you next week, bye everybody, have a good weekend.

(She goes out briskly.)

SHELLEY. It's friggin' April anyway.

*(She, **MAXINE** and **ROSE** laugh and nudge their way out, ad-libbing their goodbyes. Outside, they can be heard loudly laughing and talking as they leave.)*

*(**TINA** becomes aware that **ANDY** is hovering.)*

TINA. Yes Andy?

ANDY. I just wanted to say that I…felt better tonight. I really felt I was…what I mean is, I felt more relaxed…I mean I know I'm not very good but…

TINA. D'you know what *I* get out of these classes, Andy? Seeing people enjoying themselves. Oh sure, I like to see you all improving, it's good for you, it's good for me. But the biggest rush – the real rush – is that we're all enjoying ourselves. Right?

*(She smiles. And after a moment, **ANDY** smiles.)*

ANDY. Goodnight.

TINA. Goodnight, Andy.

*(**ANDY** moves away and, without stopping or looking back, does a little shuffle step ball change and goes out.)*

MRS. FRASER. You should be selling encyclopedias.

TINA. Done that, thank you.

MRS. FRASER. There's really not much you haven't done, is there?

TINA. Listen, if I don't sell these classes, we're both back at Unemployment, aren't we?

MRS. FRASER. Oh, you don't have to worry about me…

TINA. I'm not worrying about you, Glenda, I'm reminding you.

MRS. FRASER. In my opinion it's about time that so-called man of yours got himself a job.

(**TINA** *ignores this and wearily moves around, straightening chairs, collecting* **VIVIENNE**'s *coasters, removing her cigarettes and lighter from the wastebasket etc – all part of the routine.*)

You look worn out.

TINA. I feel worn out, okay?

MRS. FRASER. You do too much.

TINA. Do I?

MRS. FRASER. Running around, wasting your life – and for what?

TINA. Mind your own damn business.

MRS. FRASER. Fine.

TINA. My life – all right?

MRS. FRASER. I've looked after you since your mother walked out.

TINA. Yeah yeah yeah, I'm very grateful and I always will be grateful now why don't you just go wait in the car before one of us says something we'll regret.

(*They hold their look at each other. Then* **MRS. FRASER** *stands, to collect her things, but, wanting the last word, as ever:*)

MRS. FRASER. I'm telling you: you do too much.

TINA. You're right, okay?? You're right. I'm agreeing with you. I'm agreeing with you.

MRS. FRASER. Your trouble is you agree with *everyone*, madam. You let people walk all over you, especially You-Know-Who. In *my* opinion…

(*But* **TINA** *has already interrupted her with:*)

"TOO MUCH"

TINA.

I WORK TOO MUCH – I SMOKE TOO MUCH
AT THE END OF EVERY MONTH I'M KINDA
BROKE TOO MUCH
I GUESS BY NOW YOU'D THINK I WOULDA LEARNED
TOO MUCH IS NOT ENOUGH WHERE I'M CONCERNED

I LOVE TOO MUCH – I LIVE TOO MUCH
AND YES I KNOW – I KNOW – I ALWAYS GIVE
TOO MUCH
BUT EVEN WHEN THE GOING'S GETTING TOUGH
I STILL BELIEVE TOO MUCH IS NOT ENOUGH

I NEVER CARE ABOUT THE WHY AND WHEREFORE
AS LONG AS THERE IS SOMEONE I CAN CARE FOR
SOMEONE TO BE THERE FOR – THEREFORE

I HOPE TOO MUCH AND CHANCE TOO MUCH
AND EVERY NOW AND THEN GET UP AND DANCE
TOO MUCH
AND EVEN THOUGH MY FEET ARE SORE
WHILE THERE'S A TINY PIECE OF FLOOR
I'M GOING TO DANCE TOO MUCH AND THEN SOME MORE

I'M OVER-COMMITTED, TOO TIRED OR TOO BUSY
TO NOTICE I'M DRINKING TOO MUCH
AND EVERY SO OFTEN I'LL DANCE TILL I'M DIZZY
TO STOP MYSELF THINKING TOO MUCH
IT'S TIME TO CONCEDE – WHAT I WANT –
WHAT I NEED –
WHAT I CRAVE IS A DREAM I CAN TOUCH
I WANT LOVE – I NEED LOVE – MUCH TOO MUCH

*(Throughout this, **MRS. FRASER** has tried to have her say and now **TINA** ushers her out through the swinging doors.)*

(a dance break)

TINA. *(cont.)*

> I HOPE TOO MUCH AND CHANCE TOO MUCH
> AND LIVE AND LOVE AND LOSE AND DREAM AND
> DANCE TOO MUCH
> BUT EVEN THOUGH MY HEART IS SORE
> AS LONG AS THERE'S AN OPEN DOOR
> I'LL LOVE IT ALL TOO MUCH AND THEN SOME MORE

> *(She grabs her coat, bag, cigarettes, and cell phone and goes out, turning out the lights so that the gym is in darkness.)*

Scene Seven

(A coffee shop. The same evening.)
*(***ANDY*** and ***GEOFFREY*** sit with coffee mugs. They are relaxed and chatting.)*

GEOFFREY. My wife and I really used to enjoy dancing. That's how we met – at the office Christmas dance. She was with her father – my boss – sitting at the "head table." From the minute I saw her I just…I just wanted to be with her. And so I took my courage in both hands…or both feet I suppose you could say and… that was that. We used to go dancing almost every week…before we were married and…for a few years after. And then it became…just something that used to be. Then a couple of months ago I saw Tina's ad in the paper and I thought…why not? So I took the plunge and… *(he smiles)* …here I am. And you?

ANDY. Oh I go to classes all the time. I have a lot of – free evenings – what with my husband's work and my son being away at school and so I go to classes and…"improve" myself. I'm heavily into self-improvement. Tap Dancing for co-ordination…Ancient Greek for derivation…Art Appreciation for – art appreciation. *(She smiles at the memory of:)* I did a course on car maintenance once. I actually wanted the Assertiveness Class but went into the wrong room and was too scared to say anything, so if you ever want a spark plug cleaned or anything…

(They smile at each other. Pleased to be in each other's company.)

I really enjoy these evenings. Going to class and then having coffee and just – talking. I feel – very easy talking to you. The truth is… *(She almost decides not to continue, but…)* …the truth is…I miss – conversation. When I was first married we used to talk about everything. There didn't seem to be enough words for what we wanted to say, to – tell each other. Now he's away so much and his mind is so much on…I mean I don't blame him, of course I don't, it's just that I sometimes wish things could be as they were. That we were…as we were.

(a moment)

GEOFFREY. Yes. *(a little smile)* But things can never be what they were, can they? Everything changes.

ANDY. Maybe that's the reason for most of our unhappiness – we can't accept that *(and she continues directly into:)*

"NEVER FEEL THE SAME AGAIN"

GEOFFREY.

LIFE CAN NEVER BE PERFECT,

ANDY. *(speaking)* No.

GEOFFREY.

YET SOMETIMES IT'S FILLED WITH HAPPINESS,

ANDY. *(speaking)* Yes.

GEOFFREY.

BUT YOU CAN'T REBUILD THAT HAPPINESS,
FROM THE MOMENT IT'S TAKEN AWAY.

AND YOU NEVER FEEL THE SAME AGAIN
SOMETHING CHANGES
AND YOUR DREAMS ARE COMPROMISED
YOU HAD ONLY JUST BEGUN –
AND THEN IT WAS DONE
THE CHAPTER WAS ENDED.

AND YOU NEVER FEEL THE SAME AGAIN
ONCE YOU KNOW
THOSE DREAMS CANNOT BE REALIZED
AND THOUGH ALL YOUR HOPES ARE GONE
STILL LIFE CARRIES ON –
THOUGH SOMEWHAT AMENDED.

ANDY.

AND SO THE DAYS GO BY
UNSPARINGLY
THE WORLD MOVES ON RELENTLESSLY.
UNCARINGLY

GEOFFREY.

IT'S A YEAR, OR IS IT TEN?

ANDY.

AND YOU NEVER FEEL THE SAME AGAIN

ONCE YOU KNOW THE SITUATION'S FINALIZED

GEOFFREY.

SO YOU PUT YOUR DREAMS AWAY

YOU CLOSE THE BOOK

AND SAY "AMEN"

BOTH.

AND NEVER FEEL THAT WAY AGAIN

BUT LIFE CAN STILL UNFOLD EXCITINGLY

THE FUTURE WAVING HOPEFULLY

INVITINGLY

AND YOU WONDER NOW AND THEN

WHY YOU'LL NEVER FEEL THE SAME AGAIN

IF YOU CARE TO GET YOUR FEELINGS ANALYZED

IT'S MUCH EASIER TO SAY

LET'S CLOSE THE DOOR ON WAY BACK WHEN

AND NEVER FEEL THAT WAY AGAIN –

GEOFFREY. Andy… *(But whatever he was going to say, he decides against it.)* I'll get the check.

BOTH.

SAY AMEN – AND NEVER FEEL THAT WAY AGAIN

(They remain where they are. We hear the sound of rhythmically tapping shoes and the lights change.)

Scene Eight

(The YMCA gym. Two weeks later. Evening.)

*(**TINA**, notebook in hand, is going through the simple steps she will teach tonight, looking at herself in the mirror....during which she sees **LYNNE** come in. **LYNNE** wears her nurse's outfit, rainslicker over it, and carries her bag.)*

TINA. *(brightly)* Hi…I'm just going through some stuff for tonight – gotta keep one step ahead of you guys.

*(**LYNNE** gives a little smile and stands watching as **TINA** does the simple step combination. With a smile at **LYNNE** – she finishes with a brief but rapid fire little combination…)*

LYNNE. I wish I could dance like you.

TINA. You will.

LYNNE. No. Never. There's a difference…

TINA. I've been doing it for a hundred years, don't forget.

LYNNE. No, but there is. There's a difference.

(She moves to set her bag down).

TINA. Hey. Are you all right? You look a little down – not like my cheerful Lynne.

*(**LYNNE** smiles as if to indicate "I'm OK" but…)*

LYNNE. One of my old ladies died this morning. I'm on the geriatric floor this week and – well, to be honest, it's the first patient I've seen die. I didn't think I'd like – be so upset. Some nurse I am, huh? I guess what really got me was…well, nobody ever came to see her. And all last night she was trying to talk to me but…we were like – so busy. Sometimes it's really quiet but last night we were…so busy. Oh Tina, I just wish I'd…

TINA. I know, I know…

*(She moves to put her arms around **LYNNE** and they hold each other tight.)*

LYNNE. I'll have to get used to it, won't I? And I will of course I will. Which is somehow worse in a way, isn't it?

(A moment. Then **TINA** *breaks away.)*

TINA. Hey listen. I was thinking of splitting up the class tonight, one half with me, the other with you – what d'you think?

*(***LYNNE*** smiles, understanding full well, and is reaching out to touch* **TINA**'s *hand as* **MAXINE** *breezes in.)*

MAXINE. Hi Tina, howz Tina doin', hi Lynnie, howz Lynnie doin'? I have had a day you wouldn't believe, believe me.

*(***DOROTHY*** comes in.)*

Hi Dorothy, howz Dorothy doin'?

DOROTHY. Tina, is it all right if I bring my bike in? Someone tried to steal it today, and I'm kind of nervous about it.

TINA. Oh no! Yeah, sure.

*(***DOROTHY*** ducks out again and* **LYNNE** *goes to help her.)*

MAXINE. First of all the wholesaler lets me down, then I have to go see my lawyer and when I come out, no car. I've been towed. Three hours it takes, you wouldn't believe those morons.

*(***LYNNE*** holds open the doors and* **DOROTHY** *wheels in her bicycle and leans it against a wall where* **GEOFFREY** *usually changes, then goes through into the dressing room.)*

So I finally crawl home and then the neighbours start in on me. Seems The Little Wonder-Brat's been firing his BB gun out the bedroom window and the Greek guy next door's going demented because he's knocked the eye out of one of his lions. The guy's got these two stone lions either side of his driveway. The whole street's mortified. Two stone lions and the family crest above the garage… *(she indicates)* …"I Live To Serve." We all know he lives to serve, he runs the diner down on Rte. 28. He calls it an Aegean Seafare Taverna. *Please.* It's a Greek diner, trust me.

(MRS. FRASER comes in with her bag and music case.)

MRS. FRASER. Why's there a bicycle in here?

LYNNE. *(putting on her tap shoes)* It's Dorothy's.

(MRS. FRASER moves to the piano, once again depositing TINA's cigarettes in the wastebasket as:)

MRS. FRASER. I see: we're a garage now, are we?

MAXINE. It may be a garage to you, Mrs Fraser, but to me it's an oasis.

MRS. FRASER. Is that so.

(GEOFFREY comes in. He makes for his usual spot and is a little thrown to see the bicycle there. MAXINE has moved to pay TINA.)

MAXINE. Then his father comes home in one of his fabulous moods: he's had a bad day – y*ou've* had a bad day?? When I tell him about The Sundance Kid on safari he doesn't even know he's *got* a BB gun – "Why'd you let him buy one?" he says. Let him!? When have I ever been able to stop him from doing anything? He's eighteen years old, he's not *my* son he's *your* son and whenever I do try talking to him all I get is 'stop bugging me you're not my mother.' Kids. I love'em. I can't have'em but I love'em.

(ROSE and SHELLEY enter cheerily with their bags.)

SHELLEY. Hey cool, someone's left their bike.

MAXINE/LYNNE. It's Dorothy's.

SHELLEY. Shoot. I coulda used a nice bike. Just to lean on, not to ride.

(VIVIENNE bustles in.)

VIVIENNE. Hello everyone sorry I'm late.

SHELLEY. You're not late.

VIVIENNE. In fact I almost didn't make it this evening, I had Lionel calling from Santiago, Chile...

(VIVIENNE goes straight through into the dressing room. We hear a cell phone ring. It's from TINA's bag but those who have bags automatically reach for them.)

TINA. It's mine – sorry. Sorry – won't be a sec.

*(She heads to the lobby with her phone to speak privately, smiling as **ANDY** comes in through the swinging doors, holding the door open for her. **ROSE** and **SHELLEY** will move to pay **MRS. FRASER**, **GEOFFREY** has remained staring at the bicycle.)*

GEOFFREY. Why did she bring it in here?

LYNNE. It almost got stolen today so she's like kinda nervous?

*(**DOROTHY** comes out of the dressing room, changed, with her wallet, and will pay **MRS. FRASER**.)*

SHELLEY. Is that true, Dorothy – someone tried to grab your bike?

DOROTHY. Bike – yes – I know – it had the lock on and everything.

ROSE. Both my boys had theirs stolen last year.

DOROTHY. I don't know where I'd be without my bicycle.

ROSE. Call the police and what happens? Nothing.

DOROTHY. Nothing – no.

*(They put on their tap shoes etc. **VIVIENNE** comes out of the dressing room. She is wearing a skin-tight silver catsuit.)*

ROSE. Hey hey hey – look at Vivienne –

SHELLEY. Where're my shades, I need my shades!

VIVIENNE. Like it?

(She admires herself in the mirror to general approval from the women.)

ROSE. That is really – somethin' else.

SHELLEY. Maybe she'll make you one.

VIVIENNE. Oh I didn't make it – no no – I was in town this morning so I flew into the Dance Center. It was horrendously expensive but I just couldn't resist it. D'you like it, Maxine?

MAXINE. It's very nice.

VIVIENNE. *(pushing out her breasts)* It's not too, well, bold, is it?

MRS. FRASER. I'd be careful about wearing it to meet the Pope.

MAXINE. Oh I don't know: every crowd needs a silver lining.

VIVIENNE. I thought it might be a weensy bit bold.

ROSE. I say we need the man's opinion. Geoffrey – is that too bold or is that too bold?

(**VIVIENNE** *poses for him.*)

GEOFFREY. Umm…no…it's umm…

SHELLEY. Truer words was never spoke.

ROSE. Thank you Geoffrey.

(**VIVIENNE** *taps her way across to* **ANDY.** *So that they are both looking into the mirror as*)

VIVIENNE. I hope you don't mind me asking, Andy, but why do you always cover yourself up?

ANDY. *(instinctively touching her upper arm)* Why do I what?

VIVIENNE. What I mean is – you've got a nice body. In its own way.

ANDY. Really.

VIVIENNE. Really. It's long, but it's nice. It seems such a shame to wear clothes that cover it up all the time.

ANDY. I think you're being slightly rude, don't you?

VIVIENNE. I wasn't trying to be nosey or anything.

ANDY. There's nothing to be nosey about. I wear what I want to wear. Sorry, Vivienne.

VIVIENNE. But I'm right though, aren't I, Maxine?

ANDY. Oh, not *her* opinion – *please.*

MAXINE. *(ignores this)* What's that, Vivienne?

VIVIENNE. Clothes. Well, not just clothes, one's whole appearance. It's well – everything, really, isn't it?

"DEFINITELY YOU"

VIVIENNE.

IF YOU LOOK LIKE A DRUDGE
YOU FEEL LIKE A DRUDGE
ARE ALL OF YOUR CLOTHES
THE COLOR OF SLUDGE?
SAY GOODBYE TO THOSE SHADES
OF SEAWEED AND KELP
WHY NOT FIND A NEW LOOK?
WE'RE ALL HERE TO HELP

I HOPE YOU DON'T MIND
THAT SHADE IS DEFINITELY OUT
WITHOUT A DOUBT
I KNOW YOU WON'T MIND
THAT LENGTH IS POSITIVELY WRONG
IT'S FAR TOO LONG
YOU KNOW I'M ALWAYS RIGHT
IN MATTERS OF FASHION
THAT LOOK IS TOO ASHEN
YOU REALLY COULD DO WITH A HINT OF PASSION

YOU KNOW A GOOD START WOULD BE TO
REDEFINE YOUR TASTE
IF NOT YOUR WAIST
I THINK YOU COULD START BY
RAISING YOUR SIGHTS
(AND YOUR HEM AND YOUR TIGHTS)
AND THEN WE'LL FIND A STYLE
THAT'S REFRESHINGLY YOUNG AND NEW
YOU'LL NEVER KNOW TILL YOU TRY IT
AND THEN YOU JUST HAVE TO BUY IT
A LOOK THAT SAYS DEFINITELY YOU

SHELLEY. Whadda *you* say, Max – you're in the rag trade.

MAXINE. What I say is there are just two rules: always buy wholesale and never wear anything that will frighten animals or small children.

VIVIENNE.

YOU AREN'T WHAT YOU WEAR

YOU WEAR WHAT YOU ARE

MAXINE.

WHICH ARE YOU AWARE

IS SORTA BIZARRE

VIVIENNE.

IT'S NOT HARD TO ACQUIRE

SOME FLAIR AND SOME VERVE

LOOK AT ME I'VE GOT VERVE

SHEL/MAX/RS.

LOOK AT HER SHE'S GOT NERVE

MAXINE.

DON'T THINK I WOULD SAY

THAT OUTFIT'S DEFINITELY YOU

ALTHOUGH IT'S TRUE

ROSE.

ALTHOUGH I COULD SAY I'VE NEVER

SEEN A SILVER BOMB WITH SUCH APLOMB

SHELLEY.

IT LOOKS AS THOUGH THOSE SEAMS ARE STARTIN'

TO SMOULDER

ROSE.

IT COULDN'T BE BOLDER

MAXINE.

UNLESS IT HAD STRIP LIGHTS ON EACH SHOULDER

MAX/SHEL/RSE.

I HOPE YOU DON'T MIND

ROSE.

THAT SUIT IS REALLY KINDA BRIGHT

SHELLEY.

AND KINDA TIGHT

MAXINE.

I HOPE YOU WON'T MIND

SHELLEY.

A WORD OF ADVICE

ROSE.

THOUGH IT'S VERY NICE

MAXINE.

THAT GET-UP MIGHT LOOK BETTER

ON SOMEONE WHO'S TWENTY-TWO

VIVIENNE.

YOU THINK IT'S JUST TOO AUDACIOUS?

ROSE.

I THINK IT COULD BE –

MAXINE.

MORE SPACIOUS

MAX/SHEL/RSE.

A LOOK THAT SAYS DEFINITELY...

MAXINE. Just a minute, just a minute, I've got the perfect thing...the perfect thing...

(She goes to her bag and will pull out a very large and hooded sweatshirt which she will "persuade" **VIVIENNE** *into – this during)*

ALL.

A LOOK THAT SAYS POSITIVELY...

MAXINE. It's the start of a line that was never finished...

SHEL/RSE.

A LOOK THAT SAYS

MAX/SHEL/RSE.

DEFINITELY

MAXINE. Now here's the kind of schmutter that is utterly

ALL.

YOU

(And they have enveloped **VIVIENNE** *in the large sweatshirt and the hood is pulled completely over her head and they turn her upstage, and we see "Save The Whales" written on the back of the sweatshirt.)*

*(***TINA*** comes in with her cellphone.)*

TINA. Okay, listen up people – ladies – Geoffrey – if I can have your attention please.

SHELLEY. Uh-oh, this sounds nasty...

TINA. I just got a call from Liz Beckley – she runs the adult education classes – some of you maybe know her?

VIVIENNE. *(hand up)* I do.

TINA. *(with mounting enthusiasm)* Well anyway, Liz has been asked to organize a charity show for the end of July – dance groups from all over the state are taking part and she's dying for us to do the tap number. I said I'd ask you but I'm pretty sure the answer will be yes.

(General murmuring. **MRS. FRASER** *even manages to look up from her magazine.)*

So what do you think?

(They seem stunned.)

ROSE. For the end of July.

TINA. Plenty of time. No problem.

VIVIENNE. But what kind of thing would we have to do?

TINA. The same kind of thing we're doing now.

SHELLEY. Oh my gawd.

ANDY. *(putting hand up)* Would all of us have to be in it?

TINA. Only if you want to be. Anyone who doesn't, doesn't have to – but you have to tell me soon because obviously I have to come up with some kind of routine.

DOROTHY. What charity is it?

TINA. Save The Children.

MAXINE. Wouldn't you know it?

GEOFFREY. *(hand up)* When you say you'll come up with some kind of routine, umm...

TINA. It won't be anything more difficult than we've already done – you've learned to tap so let's put it together and really show them what we can do, what do you say?

VIVIENNE. Anyway, it's only for charity, isn't it?

ANDY. Yes, I mean they won't be expecting too much, will they?

TINA. Now hold it, hold it everybody…that's the wrong attitude. As far as I'm concerned, being asked is – well, it's
really sort of an honor, and what they're going to get is
the best we can give them.

MAXINE. Well, I think it's a terrific idea. I would have pre-
ferred to Save the Parents, but…

DOROTHY. We're really going to sock it to them, aren't we,
Tina?

SHELLEY. Whoa, listen to her all of a sudden.

TINA. No but she's right, absolutely right.

DOROTHY. Right – yes.

*(And now all the others are showing mounting enthusi-
asm as)*

TINA. Let'em see what we've been doing every Thursday,
yeah?

(general murmurings – more enthusiastic still)

Okay, okay enough – think about it – we've gotta move
on…Now what I want to do is go right from where we
stopped last week – all right, Glenda?

MRS. FRASER. I should have been told about this.

TINA. I only just found out about it.

MRS. FRASER. Nevertheless, I should have been consulted.

TINA. *(clapping her hands)* Okay people, get yourselves in
two lines…whenever you're ready, Glenda…and five
six seven eight…

"ONE NIGHT A WEEK"

TINA.
ONE NIGHT A WEEK WE'LL START TO REHEARSE

MAXINE. Show business here I come!

TINA.
IMPROVING EACH WEEK

SHELLEY.
WE COULDN'T GET WORSE

DOROTHY. Wait till I tell my mother!

ROSE.

> WHY DON'T WE GIVE IT A SHOT
> WHAT CAN WE LOSE?

SHELLEY.

> NOT A LOT

VIVIENNE.

> IF WE ALL TRY –

DOROTHY.

> TRY – YES

VIVIENNE.

> AND PULL TOGETHER

SHELLEY.

> AND GO AT IT HELL FOR LEATHER

MAX/VIV.

> ONE NIGHT A WEEK

LYNNE. It'll be fun, won't it?

SHEL/ROSE.

> WE'LL WORK AS A TEAM

MRS. FRASER. I don't come here to have fun

SHEL/ROSE.

> LOOK WE'RE A TEAM

ANDY. What d'you think, Geoffrey?

SHEL/ROSE.

> THAT'S BUILDING A DREAM

GEOFFREY. Well if, er…

TINA/LYNNE.

> THINK ABOUT MUSIC AND LIGHTS

VIVIENNE.

> THINK ABOUT SEQUINS AND TIGHTS

MRS. FRASER.

> THINK ABOUT SAILING SLOWLY UP THAT CREEK…

MAXINE. Faith, Mrs. Fraser – Faith!

ALL.

> IF WE BELIEVE
> WHO KNOWS WHAT ELSE WE MIGHT ACHIEVE
> ON ONE NIGHT A WEEK

> *(curtain)*

ACT TWO

(The Entr'acte ends and we hear the sound of a piano being played, slowly and unmelodically.)

(The curtain rises.)

Scene One

(The YMCA gym. A week later. The piano is now upstage right.)

(TINA is at the piano with MRS. FRASER who is moodily clumping out the rehearsal music for their show number. The class members break and stand around chatting. SHELLEY bites into a doughnut from a deli bag. LYNNE is going round with the cashbox, collecting class money. DOROTHY is wearing a pair of handknit legwarmers and a matching headband. VIVIENNE is busy scuttling around with the wastebasket. TINA listens to the clumping piano-playing as the vamp continues.)

TINA. So that's the way you're going to play it? That's the way you expect me to rehearse them?

MRS. FRASER. *(stops playing)* I need time to absorb.

TINA. We don't *have* time, Glenda, and you know it. Now don't hassle me – please – I don't need this – just go through it again, the way you know it *should* be – while I go make a quick call.

(And she makes to exit, grabbing her cell phone from the top of the piano, and – a fast afterthought – her cigarettes, before MRS. FRASER can relegate them, as usual, to the wastebasket.)

MRS. FRASER. I should have been consulted!

TINA. Yeah yeah yeah, you should have been consulted.

(She exits. **MRS. FRASER** *glares after her, then glares at the sheet music, then continues to bash out the piano vamp – which is in fact the intro to the number that follows, "DOCTOR FOOTLIGHTS" – under the following dialogue.)*

MAXINE. *(of the departing* **TINA***)* Well, that's a great start to our showbiz career…

VIVIENNE. Oh it's not a career, Maxine. We're doing this for love, not money.

DOROTHY. Love – yes.

MAXINE. Let's hope you're still saying that when the reviews come out…

ANDY. *(horrified)* Reviews?

SHELLEY. Maybe doing a show isn't such a hot idea.

*(***ROSE*** *takes off her bandana and reveals a short curly haircut.)*

ROSE. How can I face my public like this!

SHELLEY. It's growing out real nice, Rose. Very becoming, eh, Dot?

DOROTHY. Becoming – yes.

ROSE. But what it's becoming, nobody knows!

ANDY. Maybe we should tell Tina we're just not up to it.

ROSE. Jesus, I'm nervous!

LYNNE. Who isn't!

MAXINE. Feel the fear and do it anyway . . .

DOROTHY. Fear, yes. *(realizing)* What!

"DOCTOR FOOTLIGHTS"

MAXINE. *(intro verse)*
CHRISTOPHER COLUMBUS

SHELLEY. Who?

VIVIENNE.
FOURTEEN NINETY TWO

SHELLEY. Oh, yeah.

MAXINE.
>HE TREMBLED AS HE SAILED INTO THE BLUE

LYNNE. You remember, Dot!

DOROTHY. I was there!

VIVIENNE.
>HERE'S WHAT THEY ALL TOLD HIM
>TO MAKE YOUR DREAM COME TRUE

MAXINE.
>GO OUT THERE WITH PRIDE –
>AND WHEN YOU REACH THE OTHER SIDE

MAXINE/VIV.
>AMERICA IS WAITING THERE FOR YOU…

MAXINE.
>HANG YOUR HEART UP ON THAT STAR

>(*to* **VIVIENNE**) Tell her 'Ethel'!

VIVIENNE. *(a la Ethel Merman)*
>TIME TO SHOW THEM WHO YOU ARE

MAXINE/VIV.
>SO YOUR NERVES ARE IN A KNOT
>YOU GOTTA TAKE A SHOT!

MAXINE. What do you say, Shell?

SHELLEY. What I say is – what the hell!

MAX/VIV.
>ONCE YOU STEP OUT ON THAT STAGE

SHEL/LYNNE.
>YOU DON'T HAVE TO ACT YOUR AGE
>JUST GET OUT THERE AND DO YOUR BEST

MAXINE.
>– LET DOCTOR FOOTLIGHTS DO THE REST!

ROSE. Not sure my health insurance covers that…

MAXINE. Ah, but this doctor won't charge a nickel.

SHELLEY. What! There ain't no such animal!

ALL.
>DOCTOR FOOTLIGHTS
>CURES IT ALL

VIVIENNE.

FORGET YOUR STAGE FRIGHT

LYNNE. *(to* **DOT***)*

IGNORE YOUR AGE-FRIGHT

ALL.

CUZ YOU'LL GO OUT THERE

AND HAVE A BALL!

SHELLEY.

WE'RE GONNA ROCK ROUND THE CLOCK

WITH THE DOCTOR ON CALL

ALL.

TIME TO SHOW THEM WHAT YOU KNOW

LYNNE.

TIME TO SET THE WORLD AGLOW

ALL.

YOU MAY BE SCARED TO DEATH BUT ONE THING IS FOR SURE

OL' DOCTOR FOOTLIGHTS HAS THE CURE

VIVIENNE. *I* used to be fat, you know.

SHELLEY. Oh really.

VIVIENNE. Mmm. Just after I had my baby. I was nearly as big as you are.

SHELLEY. You don't say.

VIVIENNE. She's seventeen now. All she thinks about is horses. She's horse crazy, that girl.

SHELLEY. Well, keeps her off the streets, don't it.

MAXINE.

TIME TO MAKE THIS MOMENT YOURS

LYNNE.

TIME TO SOAK UP THE APPLAUSE

ALL.

ONCE YOU STEP INTO THAT SPOT

YOUR WORRIES GET FORGOT

MAXINE. Say, Andy – we went to see that play you recommended.

ANDY. Oh – yes – did you enjoy it?

MAXINE. What can I say? We didn't even understand the intermission. Come on guys, we're doing this for Tina!

ANDY. Well – as it's for charity…

ALL.

LOOK OUT SHOW BIZ HERE WE COME!
TIME TO SHOW WE'RE NOT SO DUMB
WITH GOOD OL' DOCTOR FOOTLIGHTS STANDING BY
TAKE IT STEADY AND YOU'RE READY TO FLY!

(**TINA** *comes in through the swinging doors, dumping her cell phone and cigs on the piano, and clapping her hands with*)

TINA. Okay people, let's do it. It's our first rehearsal, so we need lots of concentration. Now –

(*They pay attention and* **MRS. FRASER** *picks up her magazine to read, spies Tina's cigs, routinely drops them down into the wastebasket and continues reading. This is the first rehearsal for the show and some are looking forward to it and some are apprehensive.* **TINA** *'s attitude will be a touch brisker – more professional. They're amateurs, she's aware of their limitations, but it's a show, after all, and her name is on it.*)

(*indicating*) Rose, Shelley and Andy – I want you three at the back – no, Rose in the middle – then Maxine, Vivienne, Lynne and Dorothy – spread yourselves out so everyone can see you – but come forward a step, you're all bunched up – and Geoffrey, you come down here in front, right in front of Rose.

SHELLEY. Shame.

(**TINA** *moves among them, checking that each is in the right position and moves to the front.*)

TINA. Okay. So you're standing with your backs to the audience… (*She demonstrates, turning her back to them.*) …feet apart and perfectly still. Nothing moving. The curtains or the lights come up or whatever and you stay there, not moving, totally dead still. For four counts you do absolutely nothing.

ROSE. I like it.

(As **TINA** demonstrates the following steps, they attempt to join in with varying degrees of efficiency.)

TINA. On given counts, back line, middle line and Geoffrey turn round and face front...no, you don't move your feet and so your legs are crossed...

(They cross their legs, most of them unbalanced.)

From there you bring the right arm up, leaving the left arm down, you lift the hat and you hold it high – okay?

ANDY. (anxiously) We're having hats? I didn't hear her say anything about hats.

TINA. So that's the first two counts, okay? On counts three and four....

MRS. FRASER. (still reading) You're forgetting the canes.

TINA. (who most certainly has, her mind still being to some extent on her argument with her boyfriend) Yes, you're right, thank you, Glenda...sorry, sorry, I forgot the canes.

MRS. FRASER. You'll forget your head one of these days. (She licks a thumb, turns a page.)

ANDY. We're having canes?

TINA. So... (She demonstrates.) ...you're not standing with the left arm down, you're standing with the cane under your arm...you turn...and up with the right arm...

LYNNE. (trying it) Cane under the arm, up with the hat...

TINA. On counts three and four, middle line of four does exactly the same thing but when you turn you leave the right arm down, holding the hat low...

LYNNE. Yikes. Sorry.

TINA. So you've got the contrast between the back line being high and the middle line being low, and Geoffrey – who's on his own as a solo – is high. You got it?

MAXINE. Can I ask a question?

TINA. Yes, Maxine.

MAXINE. What do you mean – a solo?

TINA. You mean Geoffrey.

VIVIENNE. Do you mean he's going to be special or some-thing? I mean, nothing personal, Geoffrey.

GEOFFREY. No, no, I was wondering myself what…

TINA. Geoffrey's going to be special inasmuch as he's a fella and sticks out like a sore thumb, but his solo part is going to be positional rather than a lot of tapping, okay?

VIVIENNE. Oh, I see.

MAXINE. Gotcha.

ROSE. Excuse me.

TINA. Yes, Rose.

ROSE. I can think of someone else who's gonna stand out like a sore thumb.

ANDY. *(hand up)* I wonder then if Rose should maybe be at the front with Geoffrey…?

GEOFFREY. I'm very happy to change places if…

ROSE. No, no, Geoffrey – if I'm gonna be ignored, I prefer to be ignored at the back, thanks anyway.

TINA. Getting back to the "solo" business…it's a big heavy tap number, yeah? You're working as a team, there's no individuality – apart from one section where each of you in turn will move across and do a step on your own while the others are marking time – but because you're doing a step on your own, it doesn't mean that you're the superstar – there's no big solo spot, it's a team.

SHELLEY. Did you say do a step on our own?

TINA. Nobody's going to look silly, honest. You'll do what I know you can do – and they'll all think it's wonderful, trust me.

VIVIENNE. Are we all going to wear the same costume?

TINA. Oh, I think so, don't you?

DOROTHY. It's so exciting, isn't it?

MAXINE. So what kind of costume we talking about here?

ANDY. Can't we discuss all that later?

DOROTHY. Later – yes.

MAXINE. I might be able to help, that's all.

VIVIENNE. You know…I could probably make something.

MAXINE. Whatever, I don't care.

VIVIENNE. As long as we decide so I've got enough time.

MAXINE. The hats I can definitely get – sorry to bring it up, Andy.

TINA. That'd be great, thank you.

MAXINE. But the canes – I don't think so.

LYNNE. Tina, are we going to like be getting some canes? Like to practice with?

DOROTHY. Practice with – yes.

ANDY. *(hand up)* If we're going to have a cane, I think I'd like to get used to it as soon as possible.

DOROTHY. As soon as possible – yes.

TINA. Absolutely – the sooner the better – so if you could all bring one in please. Okay let's move on. So –

VIVIENNE. Are these special canes or what?

TINA. Go to a garden center, buy yourself a bamboo stick and cut it down, okay?

ANDY. *(hand up)* So does that mean for this week, we umm…

MAXINE. Pretend, sweetie – like you do with your husband. Go through the motions and make like you're enjoying it.

TINA. Oh and by the way – there's going to be some fast bouncing around and you might have bust problems so wear something good and firm.

(They all look down at their busts as **GEOFFREY** *nods wisely.)*

TINA. *(to* **MRS FRASER***)* I want four bars of solid intro and then…

MRS. FRASER. Hats and canes? You're asking for trouble.

TINA. *(generally)* Right – let's have the first four bars and make sure the intro is right on the ball – it's got to be hot, it's got to have panache, it's got to have the three T's – what are the three T's? Tits, teeth and tonsils... *(She demonstrates.)* ...you smile, you stick your chest out, you look like you're enjoying it.

ROSE. You've only got two T's, haven't you, Geoffrey?

SHELLEY. Don't worry, Geoffrey, I've got plenty, you can have some of mine.

TINA. So go find your positions... *(She moves among them, checking.)* Knees straight, everything neat, perfectly still. When you turn around, the move has to be clean, sharp – and then freeze it once you get there – and once you're there, you keep holding it, absolutely still, you don't move a muscle.

ROSE. I like it, I like it.

SHELLEY. My husband'd be good at this.

TINA. And the music goes... *(She chants to the rhythm.)* ...four for nothing...back line...middle line...Geoffrey...

(They have attempted to turn, cross-legged, on the right beat.)

Sway, sway, arm up, hat down...and let's get into this big tap number you've all been waiting for! It'll be easier with the music... Okay and here we go and...

(She repeats the same chant – and they try out the steps, clumsily, still having much trouble crossing the legs.)

Okay, back into your opening positions and we'll try it again. Quick as you can, Rose, we've got a lot to get through. Dorothy – just a little bit smaller. Shelley, can we lose the gum? I want to see your teeth, not hear them.

*(As **SHELLEY** removes the gum, **VIVIENNE** scuttles across to hold out the wastebasket to take the gum.)*

Vivienne! All right and it's five six seven eight...four for nothing...back line...middle line...Geoffrey!

(Again their attempt has been clumsy.)

TINA. *(cont.)* It's not working, is it, it's not clean enough, it looks tacky. Okay. I think the problem is that when you turn, some of you are a little off balance – so let's try it so that instead of crossing your legs – watch – you step, putting both heels down so you're nice and solid. Right back into position please and we'll do it again – other way round please Shelley – and it's five six seven eight...

(They repeat the step, with MRS. FRASER playing the simplified version of THE END NUMBER – "STEPPING OUT"– and they are chanting out the moves as each line turns...)

ALL. "four for nothing...back line...middle line... Geoffrey!"

(This time it works well and they beam with pleasure.)

TINA. That's it, way to go. Feels better, doesn't it?

(They ad lib their happy agreement, GEOFFREY looking particularly triumphant and repeating his "turn" to show his efficiency as)

Okay, moving right along – it's all stuff you know. Watch and I'll talk you through it... *(she chants, as she demonstrates)* Fred Astaire, box step box step, eight flaps bring you into one line...that's Maxine Shelley Vivienne Rose Geoffrey Andy Lynne and Dorothy.

ROSE. – the two sore thumbs in the middle.

TINA. From there, shuffle ball change, shuffle ball change shuffle ball change, six flaps and hold. Okay we'll try it with the music.

(They protest that they aren't ready.)

Come on, come on, of course you can do it –

(Before they can protest further she indicates for MRS. FRASER to start playing.)

Five six seven eight...

(But **MRS. FRASER** *is standing, facing the class with the sudden announcement.)*

MRS. FRASER. I don't suppose any of you know, and I don't suppose any of you care – but today is Irving Berlin's birthday and I for one don't intend to let the occasion pass without tribute.

(And she plays and sings a spirited version of "Happy Birthday Dear Irving." As she finishes, there is a stunned silence which is broken by:)

DOROTHY. It's *my* birthday next Tuesday.

TINA. Thank you, Glenda, congratulations, Dorothy, and it's five six seven eight...

(and **MRS. FRASER** *plays aggressively and they attempt the steps as* **TINA** *leads them, calling out the steps...and they get it hopelessly wrong, colliding into each other, shrieking their protests...and...)*

(The lights change.)

Scene Two

(The YMCA lobby. Later that evening.)

(Vivienne's bag is on the bench. After a moment, **GEOFFREY** *comes through from the gym and stands putting on his raincoat as* **VIVIENNE**, *dressed for going home, comes bustling out of the restrooms with her little plastic basket of cleaning materials.)*

VIVIENNE. Oh, hi there, Geoffrey, I thought everybody had left.

(She can't resist giving the restrooms sign a bit of a dust as...)

GEOFFREY. Tina asked me to lock up.

(He indicates the keys. **VIVIENNE** *puts her cleaning materials into her bag as...)*

VIVIENNE. Poor Tina. I don't think she's very happy, do you, Geoffrey?

GEOFFREY. I really don't see how you...

*(**ANDY** comes through from the hall and* **VIVIENNE** *continues directly:)*

VIVIENNE. Oh Andy, you're still here too? Oh that's right, you give Geoffrey a ride, don't you? Well, must run – supper to make – just a baked ham but I ran out of red current jelly for the glaze. 'Night Geoffrey, 'night Andy.

(And she is gone. **GEOFFREY** *and* **ANDY** *exchange a little smile, then* **ANDY** *makes to put on her coat...* **GEOFFREY** *helps her and their hands touch. They are both very much aware of this first moment of physical contact. So that they remain with her hand over his... and then he is moving away with...)*

GEOFFREY. I should have told you earlier...I, umm, I won't need a ride tonight – thanks.

ANDY. Oh *(disappointed but trying not to show it)* Sure. All right...

GEOFFREY. I, umm, I have to stop by somewhere.

ANDY. Sure.

(an awkward little moment and...)

ANDY. You're sure I can't…

GEOFFREY. No, I'd rather walk. I could do with some air. But thanks.

(He has made it sound light, and they again exchange their little smiles but...)

ANDY. It's not because…no, it doesn't matter…

GEOFFREY. Not because what?

ANDY. It's not because….well, sometimes I think I ask too many questions. I mean, I ask *you* too many questions.

GEOFFREY. It's not you asking the questions, it's me not wanting to face the answers. There are some things in the past I still find…. difficult.

(This moment and...)

ANDY. Well, goodnight, Geoffrey. See you next week.

GEOFFREY. Goodnight, Andy.

(A moment and she goes. So that he is alone and:)

"RIGHT!" REPRISE

FORGET THE PAST
IT'S GONE FOR GOOD
FORGET THE PAST?
I WISH I COULD

I ONLY HAVE TO CLOSE MY EYES
AND SHE'S FOREVER IN MY GAZE
THE ONLY PERSON I WILL LOVE
TO THE END OF MY DAYS

THOUGH EVERYBODY SMILED AND SAID
IT WOULDN'T REALLY LAST THAT LONG
AND AS IT TURNED OUT THEY WERE RIGHT
THOUGH THEIR REASONS WERE WRONG

GEOFFREY. *(cont.)*

> FROM THE MOMENT I LOST HER
> I LOST PART OF ME TOO
> AND THEY SAID I'D FORGET HER
> BUT IT JUST ISN'T TRUE
> AND THEY SAID THAT IN TIME THERE'D
> BE OTHER PEOPLE
> BUT FOR ME OTHER PEOPLE WON'T DO
>
> I KNOW I OUGHT TO START AGAIN
> IT'S TIME TO WALK TOWARD THE LIGHT
> BUT THOUGH SHE'S LEFT ME IN THE DAY
> SHE'S STILL THERE IN THE NIGHT
> IT'S NOT EASY TO FORGET HER
> BUT ONE DAY WHO CAN SAY I JUST MIGHT
> LET THE PAST – GO AT LAST – WHEN IT'S RIGHT…

*(***GEOFFREY*** *exits. The sound of* **MRS. FRASER** *playing* STEPPING OUT *and the sound of the class tapping is heard.)*

(The lights change and we are into…)

Scene Three

(The YMCA gym. Two weeks later.)

*(***TINA***, notebook in hand, calling out steps and encouragement, is leading* **SHELLEY**, **MAXINE**, **ANDY** *and* **VIVIENNE** *through part of the routine. They are using bamboo canes and miming the use of hats. Their canework clearly leaves a lot to be desired,* **ANDY** *dropping hers.* **LYNNE** *and* **DOROTHY** *are trying out steps together…***ROSE** *and* **GEOFFREY** *are at the back.* **MRS. FRASER** *stops playing.)*

TINA. Uh-huh, that's not bad, not bad at all…

ANDY. *(hand up)* I'm still really worried about my cane.

TINA. What's the problem?

ANDY. I don't seem to have any control over it.

TINA. It'll come, don't worry, there's plenty of time. *(She consults her notebook as…)* Shelley – it goes… *(She demonstrates.)* …Yup?

SHELLEY. The thing is, I know what it is in my head, I just can't get it through to my feet.

TINA. Maxine – you don't seem very happy with the paddling and rolling.

MAXINE. I'm delirious, darling, delirious.

TINA. Practice. Okay?

MAXINE. I never stop, I'm obsessed – I'm even doing it in bed.

DOROTHY. How can you do it in bed?

MAXINE. That's what *he* says.

TINA. Dorothy – you're still pushing too hard.

DOROTHY. Too hard – yes…

TINA. And the same goes for you, Andy – try and relax, nice and loose, okay? Rose – you know what I'm going to say, don't you?

ROSE. *(peering from behind* **GEOFFREY***)* Stop hiding.

TINA. They want to see you.

ROSE. Oh Jesus, don't remind me.

TINA. You gotta think Wow! Pow! Pizazz! If you got it, flaunt it. Geoffrey – use your ankle… *(She demonstrates.)* … pick up your toe and bang it in, pick up your toe and bang it in. Lynne – what happened to the time step?

LYNNE. Sorry. I got carried away.

TINA. And you can't hold a cane and bite your nail at the same time – it may taste good but it looks terrible. Oh yes – Rose – you're a step behind.

(**ROSE** *is sitting in front of the stage, exhausted.*)

ROSE. No, angel, I'm forty years behind.

TINA. Okay. Anything else? Well, that's it for tonight, thank you, good work guys, everyone. Looking good.

(**MRS. FRASER** *instantly strikes up the piano roll as* **TINA** *hurriedly gets her things together including her cigs from the wastebasket as*)

VIVIENNE. Canes to me!

ALL. Canes to Vivienne!

(**VIVIENNE** *will collect the canes like a school monitor and take them into the dressing room and* **DOROTHY** *and* **LYNNE** *go in after her as*)

TINA. Can someone lock up for me tonight? I'm kind of in a hurry.

ANDY. Yes. I can.

TINA. *(giving her the key)* Just push it through the mail slot – thanks, you're a dear – and Andy, you're doing fine, trust me, everything's going to be all right.

MRS. FRASER. Is that so.

TINA. Oh and Maxine – *(She mimes.)* – the hats.

MAXINE. Next week – definitely.

MRS. FRASER. It was last week definitely.

(**VIVIENNE** *bustles out of the dressing room, wearing yellow rubber gloves and holding an aerosol spray.*)

VIVIENNE. Tina…there is one thing we've been wondering…since this is going to be a real show and everything, will we be having Mrs. Fraser or real musicians?

(Everyone waits for the reaction.)

MRS. FRASER. I don't think I heard that.

VIVIENNE. I mean, all kidding aside.

MRS. FRASER. Who is this "we" may I ask?

VIVIENNE. It was just a general topic of conversation. One or two of the girls.

("The girls" turn away and studiously examine the walls. MRS. FRASER eyes them beadily.)

MRS. FRASER. I see.

TINA. *(stepping in quickly and clearly winging it)* I know what you mean, Vivienne – and the reason I haven't said anything definite yet is because I'm still waiting to hear something from Liz – it really depends on what facilities are available there – whether we have Glenda or Glenda with maybe a couple of other musicians – or whether we just use a music track – that sounds about right, doesn't it, Glenda, you've done quite a few of these shows.

MRS. FRASER. In my experience – it depends entirely on the quality of the production. *(Her tone makes it quite clear what she thinks the quality of this one is.)* I'll be in the car.

(She goes out, stone-faced.)

TINA. Yes, well, thank you, Vivienne – I really wish you'd waited until I said something – 'Night everyone – don't forget the lights, Andy.

(They ad lib their "goodnights", "see yous" etc. as TINA goes out, then turn to regard VIVIENNE in silence.)

VIVIENNE. Well, we need to know, don't we?

(She bustles back into the dressing room, unable to resist a little squirt of the aerosol en route.)

MAXINE. Well, *she* oughta be a good dancer, she sure knows how to put her foot in it.

SHELLEY. Yeah, but I have been wondering…

MAXINE. Of course we're going to have decent music – it's a show, we can't just have a piano.

ROSE. You wouldn't even hear it with us all banging around.

ANDY. Yes, but she hasn't actually said so, has she?

MAXINE. Oh, she's keeping the old girl happy – common sense.

SHELLEY So. We ready? We hittin' the Dreamaway? Whaddaya say?

MAXINE. Just want to make a quick call – see you over there.

SHELLEY. Okeydokey.

> (**DOROTHY** *and* **LYNNE** *come out of the dressing room, now changed, as*)

Howzabout you gals – y'all up for a l'il drink?

DOROTHY. *(a touch of rebellion)* I am, yes, I am.

LYNNE Can't. I wish.

> (**ROSE**, **SHELLEY**, **LYNNE**, *and* **DOROTHY** *go out with their bags.* **MAXINE** *picks up hers. A little look passes between* **ANDY** *and* **GEOFFREY** *behind her back.* **VIVIENNE** *comes out of the dressing room.*)

VIVIENNE. Oh, you are still here, Geoffrey – good. Give me a hand with that cabinet back there would you?

GEOFFREY. *(moving towards her)* Yes, sure, what's the umm…

VIVIENNE. I want to put my cleaning things away and the door's jammed. *(as they go)* It'll be those Cub Scouts probably, forcing it open with their thingamajigs – thankyousoverymoocho, Geoffrey, sorry to be a pain.

> (**GEOFFREY** *and* **VIVIENNE** *go into the dressing room.* **ANDY** *turns to see* **MAXINE** *looking at her.* **ANDY** *starts folding up chairs.*)

MAXINE. Goodnight, Andy.

ANDY. *(stiffly)* Goodnight.

(She rather pointedly turns off the main lights and moves away to start stacking chairs. A moment.)

MAXINE. You don't like me, do you?

ANDY. We are what we are. Isn't that what they say?

MAXINE. I'm asking you.

ANDY. And I'm sorry to disappoint you but I really haven't thought about it.

MAXINE. It isn't something you *have* to think about, either you do or you don't.

ANDY. All right, I don't think we have a huge amount in common, no.

MAXINE. Is that common as in common or common as in garden variety lower than low. *(She smiles.)* Forget it.

ANDY. I don't know what you want but I'm really not interested in standing here and…

MAXINE. D'you know what my family calls me? (**ANDY** *makes to move away but)* No no – you'll like this: Maxine The Mouth. From the age of two: Maxine The Mouth. So what am I saying? So what I'm saying is this…

"JUST THE SAME"

YOU'RE VERY QUIET
I'M VERY LOUD
I'M LIKE A RIOT
YOU'RE LIKE A CLOUD
I LIKE TO TALK
ABOUT THE THINGS THAT BOTHER ME
I LIKE TO SHARE MY POINT OF VIEW
AND AT THIS VERY MOMENT –
WHAT BOTHERS ME IS YOU
YOU SEEM UNCERTAIN
I KNOW MY MIND
BUT LIFT THE CURTAIN
WHAT DO YOU FIND?
UNDER THE SURFACE I'M AS SCARED AS ANYONE
MAYBE YOU FIND THAT PRETTY LAME

MAXINE. *(cont.)*

BUT LOOK HARD IN THE MIRROR
YOU'LL SEE WE'RE JUST THE SAME

AND JUST THE SAME AS YOU
I HAVE LEARNED TO CONCEAL
WHAT I FEEL DEEP INSIDE
ALL THOSE THINGS THAT YOU HIDE
AND LIKE EVERYONE ELSE
I KEEP PLAYING THE GAME
JUST LIKE YOU
LOOK AT YOU
JUST THE SAME

(music continues as)

I used to do all this dancing stuff at school. If you think I'm full of shit now you should have seen me then – Miss Twinkletoes. The Rockettes had nothing on me. I was terrific. Life was terrific – all laid out there just waiting for me to take advantage of it. A lot of years later, a lot of years of deflection – and getting most of it wrong – and I suddenly realize that the one thing I don't have any more is confidence. Big family joke: Maxine The Mouth is totally lacking in self-confidence.

COME TO THESE CLASSES
YOU CAN PRETEND
WEAR ROSY GLASSES
RIGHT TO THE END
SO IN A SENSE FOR ME THIS CLASS IS THERAPY
AND NOW I'M REALLY GLAD I CAME
AND IN TIME I'VE A FEELING YOU'LL
THINK SO JUST THE SAME

MAYBE I'M BITTER
MAYBE I'M GLAD
CHASING THE GLITTER
I NEVER HAD
SO THAT'S THE WAY I HIDE MY INSECURITY
SEARCHING FOR SOMEONE ELSE TO BLAME
SO LOOK HARD IN THE MIRROR

NOW IT REALLY
SEEMS A SHAME
CAN'T YOU SEE
LOOK AT US
YOU AND ME
JUST THE SAME

MAXINE. *(cont.)* Goodnight, Andy. Sweet dreams.

(She exits, pointedly turning the main lights back on. **GEOFFREY** *comes out of the dressing room. He pulls on his raincoat. We see he now has a Band-Aid on his finger.)*

GEOFFREY. Ready?

ANDY. I have to wait for my husband – he's picking me up at quarter after. He couldn't make it any earlier, that's why I offered to…

(She vaguely indicates "clean up".)

GEOFFREY. Oh. Sure.

(He smiles as **VIVIENNE** *comes out of the dressing room with her bag.)*

VIVIENNE. It's terrible when you have to lock everything up, isn't it? Sorry about your finger, Geoffrey – lucky I had my little first aid kit, wasn't it? We all set?

ANDY. I'm waiting for my husband.

VIVIENNE. Oh I'll wait with you. I don't mind.

ANDY. Geoffrey's already offered to.

GEOFFREY. Oh – sure.

VIVIENNE. Noo – I'm not in any rush tonight. Really. You go on, Geoffrey. Go on. Scoot!

(And she sits, her bag neatly across her knees, making it quite clear that she's staying. **GEOFFREY** *looks at* **ANDY** *who can scarcely conceal her disappointment.)*

GEOFFREY. I'll see you next week, then. Goodnight.

(They ad lib their goodnights. He goes out.)

ANDY. There was really no need for either of you to stay.

VIVIENNE. Don't be silly, it's only a few minutes…

(**ANDY** *moves to close the piano lid and then sits at the piano, her back to* **VIVIENNE.**)

To be honest, my two are both out tonight. They're off at the Performing Arts Center, some sort of concert, and they're bound to go get something to eat afterwards, they usually do. I think it's nice for a father and daughter to go out together, don't you? Your son goes to boarding school, doesn't he, Andy?

ANDY. Uh-huh.

VIVIENNE. Well – vacation soon – bet you'll be glad to have him home. You'd think they'd perk this place up a bit, wouldn't you? By the way, I'm thinking of making some curtains for the dressing room window – I can cut them out of an old pair I have. I never throw anything away, you know, I drive poor Lionel insane – I think he'd leave me if I didn't have my own work-room – just kidding, we're happy, we really are – not that I'm a prude or anything but anyone can see right in that window. I'll just go take a few measurements *(She pulls a tape measure from her bag as…)* – I've got my tape, well you never know when you'll need it!

(She goes into the dressing room. A moment. **ANDY** *sits looking down at the piano. She raises the lid, looks at the keyboard, and then with one finger picks out the melody of THE END NUMBER – "STEPPING OUT" – As she does, we hear the beep-beep of a car horn outside. She stops playing…then begins again, more rapidly…then as she begins striking the keys with her clenched fists…)*

(…and as the lights change we hear the voices of **MAXINE, ROSE,** *and* **SHELLEY** *dutifully chorusing… "that's really lousy/that stinks/that is terrible, Dorothy/ oh no, really?" etc. and we are into…)*

Scene Four

(The Dreamaway. Later that evening.)

*(**MAXINE**, **ROSE**, **SHELLEY** and **DOROTHY** who has clearly been going on and on for some time.)*

DOROTHY. Anyway, my mother and I were down by the lake, feeding the ducks and having a really nice time when all of a sudden this swan comes swimming along, you know how they do, and before I knew it it's coming out of the water trying to attack me…hissing and spitting…I was lucky to get away, well it could have broken my leg, I was absolutely terrified. I mean, they're so beautiful, aren't they? Why do they have to be so nasty?

MAX/SHEL/ROSE. *(flat)* Dunno, Dot.

DOROTHY. When I told my brother, you know what he said?

MAX/SHEL/ROSE. *(flat)* No.

DOROTHY. He said…did you know that when swans mate, they mate for life?

SHELLEY. Oh really? Huh.

DOROTHY. Still. That's what it's all about I guess, isn't it?

SHELLEY. What is? Sorry.

DOROTHY. Life.

ROSE. That is true, Dorothy. That is so true.

DOROTHY. Life. And what you want out of it.

(The others ad lib: "Absolutely"…"You said it …"You're so right, Dorothy"…"That's about the size of it" and:)

SHELLEY. Whadda *you* want out of life, Rosie?

ROSE. What you mean, what do I want out of life? I'm like everyone else, I just get on with it, deal with it. What's the point of thinking about it? If you think about it, you think about it. So I don't think about it. What do I want? Don't ask, I just might tell you…

"WHAT I WANT"

ROSE.

> WHAT I WANT
> IS NOT TO HAVE TO WORRY ABOUT
> WHAT I WANT
> IS NOT TO HAVE TO THINK ABOUT
> WHAT I WANT'S TO
> LIVE MY LIFE WITH HARDLY A CARE
> AND WHEN I GET HOME I WANT
> WHAT I WANT RIGHT THERE

SHELLEY.

> WHAT I WANT'S
> A NEW CAR IN THE DRIVEWAY AND –

MAXINE.

> WHAT YOU WANT
> IS FIRST OF ALL A DRIVEWAY

SHELLEY.

> AND WHAT I WANT'S
> A BRAND NEW WAY TO EAT MYSELF SLIM

ROSE. You're gorgeous, Shell.

SHELLEY.

> BUT WHEN I GET HOME I STILL WANT
> THE SAME OLD HIM

ROSE. You old softie.

MAXINE.

> WHAT I WANT
> IS CANDLES ON THE TABLE

ROSE.

> AND DINNER IN THE OVEN
> THAT I DON'T HAVE TO MAKE

MAXINE.

> WHAT I WANT
> IS SILK SHEETS IN THE BEDROOM
> AND SOMEBODY BETWEEN THEM
> WHO'S AWAKE

ROSE.
> WHAT I WANT'S
> TO GET MY BOY A CHANCE IN LIFE
> WHAT HE NEEDS
> A LITTLE OPPORTUNITY
> WHAT I KNOW'S
> THE KIND OF MAN THAT HE COULD BECOME
> AS LONG AS WHEN HE GETS HOME
> HE STILL LOVES HIS MOM

DOROTHY.
> WHAT I WANT
> IS JUST TO HAVE THE PROBLEMS
> THAT YOU DON'T WANT
> SOME CHILDREN I COULD WORRY ABOUT
> OR A MAN
> WHO'D MAKE LIFE WHAT I'D LIKE IT TO BE
> BUT WHEN I GET HOME
> THERE'S ONLY MY MA AND ME
> WHAT I WANT'S A

ROSE.
> CUDDLE ON THE SOFA

MAXINE.
> TO USE ALL YOUR EQUIPMENT
> CUZ IT'S STARTING TO RUST

DOROTHY.
> WHAT I WANT'S A

SHELLEY.
> BODY LIKE MADONNA

DOROTHY.
> – I'D SETTLE FOR A THIRTY-TWO INCH BUST

ALL.
> WHAT I WANT

SHELLEY.
> IS NOT TO WIN THE LOTTERY

ALL.
> WHAT I WANT

SHELLEY.
> WELL MAYBE JUST A MILLION THEN

ALL.
> WHAT I WANT'S
> A MAN WHO'S GOT SOME SPARKLE AND FIZZ
> AND WHEN I GET HOME
> I'LL KEEP LIFE THE WAY IT IS

SHELLEY. D'you know what I'd *really* like? To graduate.

MAXINE. From what?

SHELLEY. Don't care. Anywhere. Anything. Just graduate.

DOROTHY. What *I'd* really like is a new lock for my bicycle.

MAXINE. Don't reach for the stars, Dot.

DOROTHY. All right then – another sherry.

SHELLEY. *(calls)* Another sherry for the senorita!

ROSE. I tell you what *I'd* like…

> *(And she whispers to* **MAXINE** *and* **SHELLEY** *and they laugh dirtily and we are into…)*

Scene Five

(The YMCA lobby. Two weeks later.)

*(**TINA** punches a number into her cell phone, waits, holding her pack of cigarettes and lighter as if trying to decide whether to go outside and have one as...)*

TINA. Hi, it's me – so what happened? About the *job*. No no – if you were too late you were too late. Listen – Jason – I need to speak to you – no, not now, not on the phone – tonight. I'll be home around...oh. Do you *have* to see him? Yeah, okay okay – how long'll you be? Okay I've got stuff to do here so – well call me and I'll pick you up – and Jason? Please don't let me down, okay? It's important. *(listens and, rather flatly:)* Love you too.

(She turns off her cell phone.)

WHAT I WANT
IS SOMEONE TO BE THERE FOR ME
WHAT I WANT'S
THE TRUTH – WELL JUST A TASTE OF IT
WHAT I WANT'S
A MAN WHO DOESN'T WANT TO BE FREE
AND WHEN I GET HOME I JUST WANT
THAT MAN TO BE
THE KIND OF A MAN WHO WANTS
WHAT I WANT FOR ME

*(**MAXINE** comes in from outside laden with her cane, bag with shoes and a large cardboard box tied with string.)*

MAXINE. I know I know, I'm late, and I'm very sorry.

TINA. These the hats, Maxine?

MAXINE. I have had a delay you wouldn't believe, believe me.

(And they are already moving through into the gym as the lights change and we are into...)

Scene Six

(The YMCA gym.)

*(**TINA** and **MAXINE** come through from the lobby.)*

*(**ANDY**, **SHELLEY** and **LYNNE** are in a group, practicing with their bamboo canes. The bottom twelve inches or so of **SHELLEY**'s cane is covered in white paint. **DOROTHY** sits blowing her nose. She has hay fever and has a box of tissues under the chair with her bag. **MRS. FRASER** sits at the piano, reading one of her magazines.)*

MRS. FRASER. So the famous hats have finally put in an appearance, have they?

MAXINE *(generally)* Sorry – I got held up.

*(**MAXINE** will get into tap shoes as **TINA** sets her cigarettes and phone down on the piano and moves across to try to open the fire doors...then gives up.)*

TINA. Geoffrey, you couldn't open this door, could you, it's like an oven in here.

*(**GEOFFREY** will, with difficulty, get the fire door open. **MRS. FRASER** brushes the cigarettes down into the wastebasket.)*

Okay. *(She claps her hands for attention.)* I guess we can assume that Rose isn't coming tonight.

SHELLEY. I can't understand it.

TINA. What I want to do first is –

*(**DOROTHY** sneezes loudly.)*

LYNNE. Bless you.

DOROTHY. Excuse me.

*(She blows violently into a tissue. **MAXINE** will untie the box as...)*

TINA. What I want to do is concentrate on the areas where the hats are important.

GEOFFREY. Won't Rose not being here umm...

TINA. We can't worry about Rose, we don't have time, she can pick it up later. But please – if any of you can't make the class – say so.

MRS. FRASER. Excuse me.

TINA. Yes, Glenda.

MRS. FRASER. Will you be requiring some form of introduction or should I just make do with a starting pistol?

MAXINE. Ta-da!

(She triumphantly holds up a red fez with a tassle. Her face drops instantly.)

DOROTHY. That's not a straw hat.

MAXINE. No shit, Sherlock.

ANDY. I thought you were getting straw hats.

MAXINE. So did I. Holy crap, look what they've given me.

(She produces another hat: a stetson.)

ANDY. Didn't you check them?

MAXINE. I ask them for straw hats, I expect them to give me straw hats.

DOROTHY. You should have checked though, Maxine.

MAXINE. Should? What's this word "should".

GEOFFREY. *(taking out a straw hat)* Here's one.

SHELLEY. Hey, Geoffrey's found one.

DOROTHY. Well, that's something, at least.

ANDY. They'll be all right to practice with, won't they?

TINA. Not really – no – they won't.

MAXINE. *(generally)* I'm sorry – I'm very sorry.

GEOFFREY. Couldn't we use them anyway, Tina – at least we'll have the feel of actually, er…

*(He mimes removing a hat and the others ad lib their agreement. **TINA** is on the point of screaming, but – with an effort at staying calm:)*

TINA. Okay everyone, grab a hat and we'll go through it – quick as you can –

*(They move in like vultures to grab a hat – **GEOFFREY** managing to keep hold of his straw hat. **TINA** becomes aware of **MRS. FRASER** regarding her.)*

TINA. *(cont.)* Don't say it – I'm not in the mood.

*(**MRS. FRASER** purses her lips and slowly shakes her head in disdain at the proceedings. They've all grabbed a hat except **DOROTHY**. The hats are all different and totally unsuitable.)*

DOROTHY. There's one missing.

MAXINE. I don't believe it.

SHELLEY. *(wearing a fez)* Look on the bright side. If Rosie'd been here there woulda been two missing.

*(**VIVIENNE**, **ANDY**, **LYNNE**, and **SHELLEY** are more concerned with looking at themselves and their hats in the mirror.)*

DOROTHY. I don't have a hat, Tina.

TINA. You'll just have to mime it.

DOROTHY. I've been miming it all month.

TINA. Then you ought to be very good at it.

ANDY. You can have mine.

DOROTHY. No, it's all right – really.

LYNNE. We can like swap later on.

DOROTHY. No, it's all right – it doesn't matter – really.

*(**LYNNE** nevertheless gives **DOROTHY** her hat. **DOROTHY** sneezes violently into her tissue.)*

ANDY/LYNNE. Bless you.

TINA. Okay okay – everyone – come on – let's get you on the diagonal – you know your positions – fast as you can please – you'll need your cane, Shelley.

*(**SHELLEY** grabs her cane and hurries into line.)*

MAXINE. *(of the painted cane)* What's that for?

SHELLEY. Nice, huh? He used it to stir a can of paint. I've only been helped across the street three times.

TINA. Can I have a straight line please – no a straight line on the diagonal, it *can't* be that difficult. Do your army thing, will you Geoffrey, or we'll be here all night.

(**GEOFFREY** *stands vaguely to attention, thrusting out his arm, army-style, and the others measure off from him, having fun, hacking around.*)

No, you haven't left a space for Rose – try and think what you're doing, it helps.

(*The line widens as they shuffle out, leaving a gap for* **ROSE**…*and* **GEOFFREY** *crashes into* **MRS. FRASER** *at the piano, causing her to play an involuntary chord… which makes the class even more giggly.*)

GEOFFREY. Sorry. My fault.

TINA. And for chrissake stop biting your nail, Lynne – okay so it's five six seven eight…

(**MRS. FRASER** *plays and they clumsily go through the steps.*)

No, you still haven't got the hat right…

(*She takes* **DOROTHY**'s *hat and demonstrates as*)

Now watch – it goes one two three four five leg leg hat…

(*She returns the hat.*)

Do it again – five six seven eight…

(*They do it again…without much more success…and* **DOROTHY** *sneezes and* **ANDY** *drops her hat causing minor chaos down the line.*)

No no no no – do it again! Do it again! Do it again!

(*She goes out into the lobby grabbing her phone as the lights change so that we are into…*)

Scene Seven

(The Lobby…with the gym in the background. The same evening.)

*(**LYNNE** enters the lobby.)*

TINA. *(to **LYNNE**)* I need a break, okay?

"ONCE MORE"

MAKE THEM DO IT ONCE MORE
RUN THE NUMBER

LYNNE.

AND THEN?

TINA.

THEN YOU RUN IT AGAIN
TIL YOU'VE DONE IT AGAIN –
AND AGAIN

LYNNE. Like, what if they won't listen to me?

TINA.

HERE COMES CHAOS ONCE MORE
I DON'T NEED THIS – NOT NOW
LOOK I'M TIRED AND I ACHE
AND I JUST NEED A BREAK
FROM THAT ROW

AND IF VIVIENNE MOANS
AND DOROTHY SNEEZES
OR SHELLEY FALLS FLAT ON THE FLOOR
PICK THEM UP – CALM THEM DOWN –
TAKE THEM THROUGH IT – AND REVIEW IT
THEN DO IT ONCE MORE

I'LL BE THERE IN A JIF
GOT TO FIND OUT THE SCORE
I'LL BE FURIOUS IF
HE LETS ME DOWN

LYNNE. *(to the class)* Okay let's do it!

BOTH.

ONCE MORE

(**TINA** *punches a number into her cellphone, gets no reply and tries again.*)

LYNNE. *(taking the class)*

SO LET'S MOVE IT ONCE MORE
START AGAIN FROM THE TOP
LIFT YOUR FEET OFF THE GROUND
DON'T LOOK DOWN – DON'T LOOK ROUND
– AND DON'T STOP

TINA.

DON'T BELIEVE IT!

LYNNE.

ONCE MORE

TINA.

KNOW WHAT THIS IS?

BOTH.

A MESS!

TINA.

WHEN I OUGHT TO SAY –

LYNNE.

GO!

TINA.

WHEN I OUGHT TO SAY –

LYNNE.

NO!

TINA.

I SAY –

LYNNE.

YES!

TINA.

'CUZ I WANT TOO MUCH
I CARE TOO INTENSELY
I'VE NEVER BEEN GOOD KEEPING SCORE
JUST THIS ONCE – JUST FOR NOW
LET HIM BE THERE – WANTING ME THERE
ONCE MORE

LYNNE.

> LOOK THEY'RE FADING – AND FAST
> ALL THEIR MUSCLES ARE SORE
> THEY'RE TOO TIRED AND HOT

BOTH.

> I/THEY KEEP WONDERING WHAT
> IT'S ALL FOR
> IF WE DO IT
> – ONCE MORE

TINA.

> NO MORE CHANCES – THAT'S IT
> SHOULD HAVE SAID THAT BEFORE

LYNNE.

> LOOK THEY'RE READY TO DROP

TINA.

> LET HIM START –

LYNNE.

> LET THEM STOP –

BOTH.

> THERE'LL BE WAR
> IF WE DO IT
> ONCE MORE – ONCE MORE – ONCE MORE

(And at the end of the song, the lights change and we are into…)

Scene Eight

(The YMCA gym. Two weeks later.)

*(The class, now including **ROSE**, is all here, each now with a bamboo cane and different hat as before.)*

TINA. Look. I think I've made a mistake. We've been trying it for two weeks now – *(barely controlled, under her breath)* and still no straw hats – and it just isn't working, it's too complicated. Having both the hat and the cane is giving you too much to think about. I just don't think it's going to work.

MAXINE. Oh.

(She does a bit with her hat and stick, making it clear that she personally can cope.)

ANDY. *(hand up)* Can I say something?

TINA. Yes, Andy.

ANDY. Well…to be honest…I never quite understood why were were having them at all.

DOROTHY. Having what?

LYNNE. Hats and canes.

SHELLEY. It's obvious, isn'it? It's to draw attention away from our feet, right Tina?

MAXINE. Speak for yourself, hot stuff.

TINA. *(firmly)* It's not working – it's my fault, but it's not working, it's tacky, I think it should be one or the other and I think we should lose the canes.

DOROTHY. Canes – yes.

MAXINE. It's sorta late in the day, Tina.

ANDY. I thought I was getting pretty good with the cane.

DOROTHY. I've been practicing with mine like crazy.

LYNNE. So have I.

SHELLEY. Me too. When I could find it.

ANDY. What I mean is – I've learned it all –

TINA. Yes, I know you don't like things being changed Andy, but you'll have to start getting used to it – I'll be changing things all the time, that's...... Look. When you use canes, it's got to be neat and precise and absolutely positively perfect. You haven't got it yet and with the time we have left, I don't think you're going to. I know you're trying, it's not your fault, it's my fault, I put them in and now I'm taking them out – so let's lose the canes and go through it with just the hats.

(She turns away as **VIVIENNE** *collects the canes.)*

VIVIENNE. Canes to me!

ALL. Canes to Vivienne!

MRS. FRASER. I warned you you'd bitten off more than they can chew.

TINA. We'll take it from the first section without the canes...and it's five six seven eight...

(They run through the same section, using just the hats. **DOROTHY** *sneezing just when she should be doing her bit and getting out of sync. They stop.)*

ANDY. It really feels strange without the cane.

VIVIENNE. Mmm, it does feel clumsy now, I have to say.

DOROTHY. Say – yes.

ANDY. It's – with the arm not doing anything.

VIVIENNE. It's almost like you need something to get hold of.

DOROTHY. Hold of, yes.

SHELLEY. Geoffrey – I think the time has come for you to make the supreme sacrifice.

TINA. *(clapping her hands)* All right all right by this time next week you'll have forgotten all about the canes, trust me.

MRS. FRASER. Oh sure...

LYNNE. So do we keep the hats on or what?

TINA. I don't care, I really don't care – I just want to see you go through your –

*(***DOROTHY*** sneezes loudly, dropping her hat.)*

RSE/LNNE/VIV. Bless you.

MAXINE. *(at the same time)* Gesundheit.

TINA. Isn't there anything you can do about that, Dorothy?

DOROTHY. I'm sorry, it's the pollen.

TINA. Okay, okay, I just want to see you go through your solos with Geoffrey. So – Geoffrey is downstage right and the rest of you –

*(**DOROTHY** blows her nose violently.)*

– the rest of you in a big V. Come on come on – so – you're all marking time –

LYNNE. Can I say something, Tina?

TINA. Yes, Lynne.

LYNNE. I've been thinking, Tina – and wondering if – like when we do this section – we could all like maybe do something different. I know it's important that we're a team and everything but I just thought this might be like the one moment where we could all do something like – you know, individual.

(vague rumblings of agreement from some of the others)

TINA. I see.

LYNNE. Well. What I meant was, seeing as how Geoffrey's the only man and the rest of us are, you know – whether we couldn't maybe all have like a different relationship with him. Only in this section, I mean.

TINA. *(flat)* What do you mean, Lynne, a different relationship?

MAXINE. I know what she means Tina, because I've been working on a little something myself – just a suggestion, naturally.

TINA. Naturally. So who else has just a suggestion?

*(Suddenly all the others, apart from **GEOFFREY** and **ANDY**, are chipping in, as they turn to each other in pairs to try out ideas that hit them… "If I did this, then **GEOFFREY** could…" …"I think it would look really cool if…." etc. and suddenly:)*

TINA. Shut up! All of you, shut up!

(They stop, stunned by her outburst.)

You've each got two bars solo with Geoffrey. Go get with him on your own and work out what you want to do – bearing in mind what you *can* do, not what you *think* you can do, which believe you me, is something quite different. You've got five minutes.

(Snatching up her cigarettes from out of the wastebasket, she exits into the lobby. A moment.)

MRS. FRASER. I hope you're all very pleased with yourselves.

(She gets up and goes out after **TINA.***)*

LYNNE. It was just a suggestion.

DOROTHY. Wow. She's really stressed.

VIVIENNE. It's not like Tina, she's been picking on us all night.

MAXINE. She's been picking on us for the last two weeks.

SHELLEY. Well, let's face it, we *have* been goofin' off a lot.

*(***DOROTHY*** sneezes.)*

That doesn't help either.

DOROTHY. I can't help it…

MAXINE/SHELLEY/ROSE. *(chorus)* …It's the pollen – yes.

GEOFFREY. I think she's probably worried we're going to let her down.

DOROTHY. Down – yes.

GEOFFREY. I mean…whatever we do reflects on her as a teacher, doesn't it?

LYNNE. I just thought it would be a good idea, that's all. I didn't mean to like interfere or anything.

ANDY. Well, what should we do? We can't just stand here.

MAXINE. Okay – who's gonna start?

SHELLEY. Start what?

MAXINE. Doing something with Geoffery.

SHELLEY. Who wants to do somethin' with Geoffery?

(vague murmurings of indecision)

ANDY. Oh look – I'll go first, I don't care.

SHELLEY. Go on, Andy, go for it, babe.

ANDY. Well, someone's got to start, haven't they? Geoffrey?

GEOFFREY. Umm…yes…what did you er…

*(They move away to talk and try out little steps, working it out together, as the others split into groups. **DOROTHY** and **LYNNE** work together, **DOROTHY** taking the man's part as)*

VIVIENNE. It's not like Tina though, is it?

SHELLEY. Maybe she had a fight with hubby.

VIVIENNE. I don't think they're married actually – I think they just live together.

SHELLEY. How shocking.

VIVIENNE. And reading between the lines, I think he gives her a pretty hard time. *(more "confidentially")* From what I hear, he's no great shakes in the finance department.

SHELLEY. How do you know all this stuff, Vivienne?

VIVIENNE. People talk to me. Probably because I'm such a sympathetic listener.

*(but **MAXINE** is nudging them with)*

MAXINE. Take a look at Fred and Ginger.

*(They turn to look at **ANDY** and **GEOFFREY** who are trying to do a step, very clumsily. **ANDY**'s back arched as he bends her backwards.)*

I wonder what kind of relationship she's got in mind.

*(**TINA** enters – discarding her cigarettes as usual on top of the piano as she passes – followed a moment later by **MRS. FRASER** who moves to sit at the piano, not looking at anyone, ignoring the cigarettes. The class waits as **TINA** moves to the front.)*

TINA. So?

LYNNE. So…not so hot, really…

TINA. Okay. You can't do it for yourselves, you have to accept that I'm the one who tells you what to do. Okay? We happy with this?

LYNNE. I wasn't trying to…

TINA. It's probably not a bad idea that each of you does something different. I'll bring some ideas in next week and you can each work on them individually with Geoffrey.

(*We get their pleased if somewhat surprised reactions as:*)

And let me just say this once. I lost my temper, I shouldn't have and it won't happen again. Okay? Now let's get going…

VIVIENNE. No, it was all our fault, Tina, and we're really really and truly truly sorry.

TINA. Yes, all right Vivienne, thank you.

(*They all gather around her, talking at the same time.*)

SHELLEY. We've been giving you nothing but grief.

MAXINE. And with the hats being all wrong.

ROSE. And me missing a class.

DOROTHY. Class – yes.

GEOFFREY. And not being able to do the, um, canes.

ANDY. We know it's important to you.

SHELLEY. We were just being stupid and silly.

LYNNE. I think it's like we're all kind of nervous.

DOROTHY. Nervous – yes.

ANDY. You've every right to be upset.

VIVIENNE. Honestly, we do understand, Tina.

(*It has all come quickly and loudly so that* **TINA** *has put her hands to her ears and…*)

TINA. No, you don't understand! I'm pregnant, for Chrissakes and I don't want to be – can you understand that?

(*Suddenly spying her cigarettes on the piano, she snatches them up and hurls them down into the wastebasket.*)

(This moment. They are all stunned into silence. Even **MRS. FRASER** *has reacted.)*

TINA. *(cont.)* Okay, let's take it right back from the top… you know your positions.

(They obediently move into their opening positions…into the two lines with **GEOFFREY** *at the front, their backs to us)*

When you're ready, Glenda, and it's five six seven eight…

*(***MRS. FRASER*** *plays and they begin to dance…the back line, middle line and then* **GEOFFREY** *turning to the front. The tempo of the playing and the way they dance reflect the stunned mood of the moment, so that they turn and go into their opening steps like lifeless puppets, no expression on their faces…and they continue dancing like this for a moment and the lights change as every-one other than* **TINA** *and* **MRS. FRASER** *forms into a line downstage and, at the same tempo, exit still in the line, downstage right…and we are into…)*

Scene Nine

(The YMCA gym. A little later the same evening…)

*(**TINA** sits on the floor, **MRS. FRASER** sits on a nearby chair looking at her. There is a discreet tap at the lobby door and it opens and **LYNNE** sticks her head in with…)*

LYNNE. Goodnight, Tina.

*(And she withdraws her head and the door is closed. **TINA** fiddles distractedly with her pack of cigarettes as there is another discreet tap at the door and **SHELLEY** sticks her head in.)*

SHELLEY. Goodnight, Tina.

*(She withdraws, closing the door. Half a moment, then another discreet tap at the door and **MAXINE** sticks her head in).*

MAXINE. Goodnight, Tina.

(And she withdraws, closing the door. Silence a moment and then…)

MRS. FRASER. *(gently)* What are you going to do?

TINA. I don't know, Glenda. I don't know.

*(Another tap on the door and this time it is **ROSE** who sticks her head in.)*

ROSE. Goodnight, Tina.

(And she withdraws, closing the door.)

MRS. FRASER. Have you told him?

TINA. Not yet. No.

*(**DOROTHY**, wearing all her cycling gear and crash helmet, comes out of the dressing room and moves straight to **TINA** to say something nice but:)*

Goodnight goodnight goodnight!

*(**DOROTHY** almost jumps out of her skin and exits as quickly as she can into the lobby. A moment, then both **TINA** and **MRS. FRASER** start to smile, and then chuckle at the sight of poor **DOROTHY** and then…)*

MRS. FRASER. *(still gently)* If you want this child, if you're going to go through with it – leave him.

*(*TINA *looks at her.)*

Face it. He hasn't got an ounce of responsibility in him. You have this child and sooner or later you'll be bringing it up on your own and you know it. So spare yourself the heartache: leave him.

*(*TINA *gives a wry little smile and...)*

TINA. Just one problem there, Glenda: I love him.

(this moment and...)

Two minutes, all right?

(A moment and **MRS. FRASER** *moves to the lobby doors and...)*

MRS. FRASER. Just make sure that for once in your life you do what's best for you.

(And she goes out. This moment and...)

"TOO MUCH"

TINA.

I NEVER CARE ABOUT THE WHY AND WHEREFORE
AS LONG AS THERE IS SOMEONE I COULD CARE FOR
SOMEONE TO BE THERE FOR – THEREFORE

I FAIL TOO MUCH
I FALL TOO MUCH
AND EVERY NOW AND THEN YOU KNOW
IT'S ALL TOO MUCH
AND IN THE END I'M REALLY NOT THAT TOUGH
I'VE DONE TOO MUCH
AND NOW....

(speaking) I've done enough

(The lights change and we are into...)

Scene Ten

(The YMCA gym. Three weeks later. June.)

(The fire door is open. All the class are wearing striped blazers, some are wearing straw hats, but not MAXINE.)

(MRS. FRASER enters, imperiously indicating for GEOFFREY to follow her, which he does, carrying a card table which he sets up downstage left as ANDY sits tying her tap shoes which have been dyed black. She has a bandage around her hand and wrist. She is even more edgy than usual tonight. MAXINE has brought a pile of fishnet tights which she distributes as VIVIENNE kneels, pinning up SHELLEY's blazer. LYNNE and ROSE decide to exchange their blazers to see if they fit better. GEOFFREY will go get a chair for MRS. FRASER to sit at the card table.)

VIVIENNE. You have to stand still, Shelley.

SHELLEY. It's not me, honest, it's my body.

MAXINE. Geoffrey – you should have a carnation, remind me to bring you a carnation.

DOROTHY. *(nudging GEOFFREY)* Isn't it exciting?

(TINA comes in through the swinging doors.)

TINA. While I remember – has everyone ordered their tickets?

(general indications of yes and no)

Well, the good news is they're going pretty fast so anyone who hasn't, can you do it now, please?

(DOROTHY and ROSE move to MRS. FRASER who notes their ticket orders as...)

LYNNE. Do we know about next week yet, Tina?

TINA. Oh – right – thanks, Lynne. *(generally)* The only time we can have the gym here next week for an extra rehearsal is Tuesday.

MRS. FRASER. *(to DOROTHY re: tickets)* How many?

DOROTHY. Nine.

MRS. FRASER. Nine…is that with bicycles or without?

DOROTHY. All my co-workers are coming from the office. They're really looking forward to it.

MRS. FRASER. I can imagine.

TINA. So Tuesday's A-OK with everyone?

(Everyone makes noises of agreement. **ANDY** *has hastily consulted her appointment book.)*

DOROTHY. I'll have to get a sitter but I'm sure I can work it.

ROSE. Is it for your mother?

DOROTHY. Mother – yes.

ROSE. If you want, I can ask my daughter.

DOROTHY. Oh I'll be fine, but thank you, Rose. She's just a little bit funny, my mother. You know – a little bit old-fashioned.

ANDY. Oh dear. That's the 19th.

TINA. Is that a problem?

ANDY. I've got a meeting on the 19th. No, no, it's all right, I can cancel.

MAXINE. *(to* **LYNNE***)* Always a crisis for The Drama Queen…

LYNNE. *(quietly)* You really shouldn't say stuff like that, she can't help it, can she, she's…

TINA. We're all okay then? Lynne?

LYNNE. Uh-huh. I'll get someone to sub for me.

GEOFFREY. So that's just two more rehearsals.

ROSE. *(holding her stomach)* Don't say that.

TINA. And the Dress on the 22nd.

DOROTHY. That's in the big auditorium?

TINA. That's in the big auditorium.

ROSE. Oh Jesus – just thinking about it turns my stomach.

TINA. And don't forget – it's full costume, full makeup, the works.

VIVIENNE. I have to remember to get my hair done.

DOROTHY. I don't think I'll have time.

MAXINE. Borrow Rosie's wig.

ROSE. Sure – if the cat's finished with it.

(Up on the stage, TINA talks to VIVIENNE about the blazers as MAXINE, SHELLEY and ROSE talk together. LYNNE takes up her iPod-type portable music player, puts on headphones and a straw hat and practices quietly on her own. DOROTHY joins in and LYNNE lets her listen in on the headphones as ANDY moves to GEOFFREY who has taken a sheet of paper from his suit pocket and is reading it.)

ANDY. You haven't ordered any tickets.

GEOFFREY. No, there isn't really anyone I, um... *(He smiles.)* Not that I'm too sorry.

MRS. FRASER. Geoffrey.

(She indicates for the table to be cleared away.)

MAXINE. So why don't I suggest it?

ROSE. Yeah, go on – ask Tina.

(MAXINE moves to speak to TINA and VIVIENNE, so that these three are up on stage as)

ANDY. Most of my friends are coming whether I want them to or not.

GEOFFREY. *(smiling)* Oh.

ANDY. God knows what they expect. Or want to expect. Anyway. They'll have something to talk about, won't they?

TINA. I really hadn't thought about it.

VIVIENNE. It would be fun though.

TINA. *(generally)* How would everyone feel about having a little party afterwards?

VIVIENNE. Just a little wine and some crudites or something.

MAXINE. Yes? What d'you think?

(They generally confer as...)

MRS. FRASER. I know what I think.

ANDY. *(to GEOFFREY)* I can't imagine anything worse.

VIVIENNE. I could do my Stuffed Baby Potatoes.

LYNNE. Where would we have it?

MAXINE. My place – yeah. Why not.

ROSE. You mean just us.

MAXINE. No – bring whoever you want.

DOROTHY. You mean like a real party.

MAXINE. Why not. I'll get Young Superslob to clean the barbecue.

LYNNE. Sounds great.

DOROTHY. Great – yes. If it doesn't rain.

MAXINE. So he'll get wet. With his personality, who'll notice?

VIVIENNE. I could do my Peanut Chicken Satays.

(They generally confer as...)

ANDY. *(to* **GEOFFREY**. *Taking the plunge)* My husband won't be here that weekend, he's away with my son. I thought maybe we could …I mean, instead of a party, I thought you might like…well, to maybe go get something to eat or something. *(And already she's embarrassed at her forwardness and)* …Only if you want to, of course, I'm not trying to…

MAXINE. So we're all set? Andy?

ANDY. Well, I'm not sure actually – I did vaguely promise someone that I'd um…

(She looks at **GEOFFREY** *as...)*

MAXINE. Whatever – Geoffrey?

GEOFFREY. If that's what everyone's doing – yes, sure Maxine. Thank you.

TINA. Okay people, we'd better get going or we'll have nothing to celebrate.

*(***ANDY** *stands, totally stunned, as the others talk in busy little groups,* **DOROTHY** *going to her purse to take out a tissue to blow her nose,* **TINA** *sitting to put on her tap shoes.* **GEOFFREY** *turns to see* **ANDY***, aware how she is feeling, and moves to her.)*

GEOFFREY. Andy, I think perhaps you misunderstood my...

ANDY. *(stiffly)* No, I think it's *you* who misunderstood, Geoffrey.

(And she moves away from him as...)

MRS. FRASER. *(looking up from her magazine)* Have you told him yet?

TINA. What?

MRS. FRASER. The baby.

TINA. I don't have to, thanks.

MRS. FRASER. I see. False alarm was it?

TINA. Something like that.... *(and she is quickly on the move with:)* You'll need the hats, everyone. There's just one change I want to make and from then on we'll keep running it until it's really clean and tight – okay – can we have the music tracks please, Lynne?

LYNNE. What? Oh yeah, sure.

(She fiddles with her iPod-type music player.)

MRS. FRASER. Do I take it that my presence is no longer required?

TINA. There isn't really anything for you to do tonight, Glenda.

*(**LYNNE** gives **TINA** the iPod, who plugs it into a small sound system/set of speakers.)*

Thanks – if you want to stay, great, but it's up to you.

MRS. FRASER. I'm quite capable of occupying my time elsewhere, thank you.

TINA. Fine.

MRS. FRASER. Just so long as I know.

*(She collects her things. **ANDY** now looks totally withdrawn.)*

TINA. *(moving to **ANDY**)* You going to be okay, Andy?

ANDY. Oh – yes – *(she fingers the bandage)* – it's just a slight sprain.

*(**MRS. FRASER** is ready to leave.)*

TINA. Goodnight, Glenda – thank you.

VIVIENNE. Are you going, Mrs Fraser?

(**MRS. FRASER** *makes a bristling exit.*)

Oh, she's not staying?

TINA. *(clapping her hands)* Okay – listen up. The first thing I want to say is: you're all still looking at the floor.

MAXINE. All of us??

TINA. Most of you – anywhere but out front – they want to see your face not your roots – and *smile* – if you don't enjoy it, they won't enjoy it, you know?

DOROTHY. The three T's.

ANDY. *(hand up)* You said you wanted to change something.

TINA. It's only one step, don't panic. Okay, we'll have a look at that first. It's just before the last section – I want to add hats – *(She takes one of their hats.)* – may I? It goes – *(She goes through the movement with the hat, chanting the step.)* – Okay? Try it.

(*She returns the hat and repeats the step and they go through it…and* **ANDY** *gets it wrong and drops her hat.*)

Okay?

VIVIENNE. Tina.

TINA. Yes, Vivienne.

VIVIENNE. What happens if someone drops their hat?

TINA. Good point. If you drop your hat – leave it. Whatever you do, don't try and pick it up – just leave it, okay?

VIVIENNE. Yes, I thought so.

ANDY. What you mean is, if *I* drop my hat.

TINA. No, if anyone…

ANDY. You mean me. That's what you meant, didn't you, Vivienne?

MAXINE. Don't be so touchy all the time.

ANDY. I didn't ask for your opinion, thank you.

ROSE. Come on, come on, chill, ladies.

TINA. We've got plenty of time to work on it, plenty.

LYNNE. Yeah, like don't worry, Andy.

TINA. Okay? So it's…

(She begins to go through the step again but…)

ANDY. I'm sorry but I really want to have this thing out.

TINA. All right, Andy – what's the problem?

ANDY. I know exactly what you're thinking. All of you.

MAXINE. Gimme a break.

ANDY. You don't think I should be in it, you think I'm letting you down.

*(General ad-libbing… "Don't be silly, **ANDY**"… "Why should anyone think…" etc. **TINA**, knowing she's got trouble, turns, braces herself against the piano a moment, has a sip of Coke, then turns back as…)*

LYNNE. You're like really good, Andy.

ANDY. *Please.*

DOROTHY. You are, you're really really good.

ANDY. I am not good. I am not – good.

TINA. Andy…

ANDY. *(wretchedly twisting her hat in her hands)* I don't know why I'm here, I don't know why I come, I can't do it, I can't *do* it.

VIVIENNE. But that's what we all admire about you, Andy.

TINA. Vivienne…

VIVIENNE. The way you try so hard.

SHELLEY. Oh, jeez…

TINA. Let me handle this, will you, Vivienne?

VIVIENNE. Well I'm only trying to be helpful.

ANDY. I don't want you to be helpful – I'm sick and tired of you being helpful, you stupid stupid woman!

TINA. *(gently)* All right, Andy, all right…

VIVIENNE. I really don't think there's any…

ANDY. You were just the same at the last class you went to – you didn't leave because you didn't like the teacher, you left because they asked you to leave – because they couldn't stand your goddamn interfering all the time – well I'm sick of you, I'm sick of this, I'm sick of all of it.

(Close to tears, she drops her hat, which only serves to increase her misery as she looks down at it.)

Oh – fuck.

*(She hurries into the dressing room. **TINA** goes after her. **GEOFFREY**, aware that **ANDY**'s distress is in no small way due to his rejection of her, has turned to watch her go, so that his back is towards us throughout the following.)*

VIVIENNE. That isn't true as a matter of fact. I left because I wanted to leave.

ROSE. Yeah, all right all right Vivienne.

MAXINE. I tell you, if this show ever gets on, I'll eat my hat.

DOROTHY. If it ever arrives…

VIVIENNE. I can't help it if certain people…

SHELLEY. D'you mind if I ask you something, Vivienne: why don't you just put a sock in it once in a while?

*(**ROSE** nudges **SHELLEY**, miming "leave her" as)*

MAXINE. Listen – it was bound to happen – it's been brewing for weeks.

ROSE. She's one very nervous woman.

LYNNE. Yeah, well maybe she has like a good reason.

DOROTHY. She swore.

MAXINE. She'll be all right when she's had her little cry.

LYNNE. You think so.

MAXINE. I certainly hope so, darling.

VIVIENNE. I suppose you think I should go apologize.

SHELLEY. *(a warning finger)* Don't you dare.

*(**VIVIENNE** sits as)*

MAXINE. Okay gang – so what're we gonna do?

LYNNE. There's nothing we can do.

MAXINE. I don't mean her.

LYNNE. No, you wouldn't…

MAXINE. What does that mean?

LYNNE. Oh – nothing.

> *(She sits.)*

MAXINE. Oh I get it: Truth or Dare time. Okay – come on. Anyone else got something to say? We've got nothing else to do, why not? Rose? Dorothy?

ROSE. Geoffrey – come the man, come the moment.

> *(And for the first time,* **GEOFFREY** *turns and)*

GEOFFREY. What?

ROSE. Exert the masculine authority.

GEOFFREY. Yes, well I… *(He takes up* **ANDY***'s fallen hat.)* …I really don't think we…she'll obviously…I mean, after all, as Maxine said…

SHELLEY. *(flatly)* Let's hear it for the voice of authority.

GEOFFREY. *(rising slightly)* I really don't think we should involve ourselves…

MAXINE. No, of course you don't – but then you don't think it's right to get involved in anything, do you Geoffrey?

GEOFFREY. Not if it's none of my business – no.

MAXINE. I get a lot of people like you in my shop, they look but they never buy.

GEOFFREY. I find that very surprising with you behind the counter.

MAXINE. *(pointing)* Sharp.

GEOFFREY. Listening to you every week, I've had a good teacher.

MAXINE. And there's me thinking you just liked being with the girls.

GEOFFREY. You know nothing about me. Nothing.

MAXINE. So educate me – what's there to know?

ROSE. *(stepping in brightly)* Okay my turn. Anyone who wants to take a shot at *me* – fire away.

SHELLEY. Whoa – big Mama's joined the fray.

ROSE. No one?

SHELLEY. We only discuss your many and colorful faults behind your back.

ROSE. *(pseudo-shock)* No…

SHELLEY. 'Fraid so.

ROSE. Well don't say I didn't offer.

MAXINE. Sit down, Rose, your roots are showing.

*(***VIVIENNE*** has been occupying herself by pointedly going through her purse. ***ROSE*** moves to sit next to her.)*

ROSE. So how many've you got coming, Vivienne?

VIVIENNE. Pardon me? Oh – sorry – just my husband and daughter.

ROSE. That'll be nice.

VIVIENNE. *(brightening)* Yes, they're looking forward to it. Are yours coming?

ROSE. Just my daughter. My husband says he prefers to wait for the "video."

SHELLEY. Whyn'tcha come with us to The Dreamaway later, Geoffrey?

GEOFFREY. *(smiling slightly)* Oh…Yeah?

SHELLEY. Yeah. Come on, we'll all go get ourselves a beer.

*(***VIVIENNE*** is showing ***ROSE*** a photo album she has taken from her bag.)*

VIVIENNE. Yes, she is like me, isn't she? *(She smiles at the photo.)* She isn't Lionel's daughter, he adopted her, I was married before, see, and – well I was very young and it didn't last. I met Lionel in Chicago, he was there for the Farm Machinery Convention and I was working in this club. I didn't want to but I had my baby to support – it was very respectable – but some of the women…you know. He was such a gentleman, Lionel. He still is. Well, you can see.

(*LYNNE crosses to* **MAXINE** *and sits next to her. The following will be overheard by* **GEOFFREY**.)

LYNNE. *(quietly)* Andy was in the ER yesterday. I didn't see her myself – I saw her name on the chart when it came down from X-ray – then later on I heard them talking about her. They don't think she like just sprained her wrist – she's been there before. They think it's her husband. They think he, like – hits her.

MAXINE. Oh Christ.

(*We see* **GEOFFREY**'s *stunned reaction.*)

ROSE. Shell – have you seen Lionel?

(*VIVIENNE takes the album for* **SHELLEY** *to see.*)

VIVIENNE. He's a lot older than me of course – well I was only nineteen but we had an incredible time, incredible. It was him who taught me all about how to dress and everything – well, he has a lot of entertaining to do, a lot of people from Europe and places and they know all about those things, don't they? And he sent me to cooking classes and oh, everything. He said "You don't want me to be ashamed of you now, do you?" He says some terrible things sometimes but it's only his sense of humor – you know – very dry. We went everywhere together, he looked after me so well and he was a wonderful lover, wonderful. I'd only been with my husband before and he was – well, he wasn't very considerate. But Lionel was wonderful. Of course, he's almost sixty now, so it's not so – you know. And he thinks the world of Louise. She's seventeen now, Lionel says she's exactly like I was when he first met me. They go everywhere together, theaters, concerts, everywhere. I don't care, I've got plenty to do and I enjoy making a nice home for them and anyway, they talk about things I don't really understand. She wants to go off and work in England but Lionel isn't sure, he really worries about her. Well, she is only a child still, isn't she?

(*The moment is held.*)

*(**TINA** comes out of the dressing room. All except for **VIVIENNE**, look to her. She tries to make it sound as light as possible as)*

TINA. She's umm, she's okay but she's still a little, you know, upset. I think maybe we should, ummm, call it a night, okay? So I'll umm, I'll see you all next Tuesday and we'll er, we'll really get our act together. Okay? Thanks.

*(And she widens her smile and they quietly start to leave and we will focus on **VIVIENNE**…and then **TINA**…and then **ANDY** as she comes out of the dressing room and we are into…)*

"LOVING HIM"

VIVIENNE.
>HOW DO YOU LOVE A MAN
>WHO FILLS YOU FULL OF DOUBT?
>HOW DO YOU LOVE A MAN
>WHO TURNS YOU INSIDE OUT?
>WHO QUESTIONS EVERY WORD
>WHO MAKES YOU FEEL ABSURD
>WHO UNDERMINES YOUR SENSE OF SELF-REGARD
>LOVING HIM IS EASY – LOSING HIM IS HARD

TINA.
>HARDLY A DAY GOES BY HE DOESN'T BREAK YOUR HEART
>HOW DO YOU LIKE A MAN WHO TEARS YOUR LIFE APART?
>A MAN THAT YOU CAN TRUST
>TO TURN YOUR HOPES TO DUST
>YOU'D THINK HE WOULD BE EASY TO DISCARD
>BUT LOVING HIM IS EASY – LIKING HIM IS HARD

ANDY.
>HOW DO YOU LEAVE A MAN
>WHO FILLS YOU FULL OF DREAD?
>HOW DO YOU LEAVE A MAN
>WHO LIVES INSIDE YOUR HEAD?
>WHOSE TAUNTS WILL NEVER CEASE
>WHO'LL NEVER GRANT YOU PEACE
>WHOSE EVERY ACTION LEAVES YOU
>SLIGHTLY SCARRED?
>LOVING HIM IS EASY – LEAVING HIM IS HARD

ALL.

> LOVING HIM – LOVING HIM
> IT'S NOT MY LIFE'S AMBITION
> LOVING HIM – LOVING HIM
> IT'S A CONDITION
> IT'S NOT WHAT I DO – JUST WHO I AM
>
> HOW DO YOU LOVE A MAN
> WHO PAINTS YOUR FUTURE BLACK?
> HOW DO YOU LOVE A MAN
> WHO CANNOT LOVE YOU BACK?
> YOU LEARN TO WALK AWAY
> AND LOVE YOURSELF TODAY
> BUT EVEN WHEN THE DOOR IS LOCKED AND BARRED
> LOVING HIM IS EASY –

VIV.

> LOSING

VIV/TINA.

> LIKING

VIV/TINA/ANDY.

> LEAVING HIM IS HARD
>
> *(The curtain comes in and we are into...)*

Scene Eleven

(A local auditorium. The night of the dress-rehearsal, a week later.)

(The curtain remains down.)

*(**MRS. FRASER** enters from the stage right wings, wearing her coat and hat, carrying a hand microphone and with her purse over her arm. She moves importantly to center and looks up towards the back of the auditorium:)*

MRS. FRASER. *(her grandest voice)* The Tina Tatowski Tappers, Item Number Six.

(no response)

Can't you hear me out there or what?

MAN'S VOICE. *(on microphone distort)* Yeah, all right, all right, I hear you.

MRS. FRASER. Might I be informed of what's happening?

MAN'S VOICE. Gary here's been having a little trouble.

MRS. FRASER. Gary isn't the only one. How long is it going to be?

MAN'S VOICE. Uh, we've had nine sugar plum fairies, three country and western and A Night In Old Vienna. We're doing our ever-lovin' best, ma'am.

*(**TINA** pushes her way through the center of the curtains).*

MRS. FRASER. Where've you been?

TINA. Trying to get a hold of Andy.

MRS. FRASER. She's still not here?

TINA. No – *(and, immediately changing the subject)* – listen, you couldn't go see if there's some coffee or something, could you?

*(She takes the microphone from **MRS. FRASER** who exits haughtily via the stage right wings as **TINA** looks up towards the unseen man and...)*

Okay, so like I said – I want to start with the spot and then I want the spot to widen and –

MAN'S VOICE. *(off)* You want a follow spot, you got it babe. Y'already told me.

TINA. And so then –

MAN'S VOICE. *(off)* – you want the cyc and boom to start, and in with the spot, and take the front of house down and then the other spot. Next?

TINA. *(with a flat smile)* And one more notch up on the sound – yes?

MAN'S VOICE. *(off)* For you doll-face, the world.

TINA. Okay, everyone – opening positions please.

(We hear the dancers hurrying on in their tap shoes and suddenly the opening bars of the music strike up and panic breaks out behind the curtain.)

Not yet not yet!

(The music stops.)

MAN'S VOICE. *(off)* Our mistake, ladies, sorry, whenever you're ready.

TINA. Say when you're ready, Lynne.

(Some more scuffling from behind the curtains and then a plaintive)

LYNNE. Ready…

TINA. Ready when you are.

MAN'S VOICE. *(off)* Five seconds.

SHELLEY. Oh my gawd…

(A brief moment…and the music strikes up…and the curtain rises we are into OUR PENULTIMATE ROUTINE OF "STEPPING OUT" with **TINA** *assisting from the side by calling out steps etc.* **ANDY** *suddenly hurries on, much to the relief of the others, and takes her place in the line. During the routine,* **DOROTHY** *spins off, clutching the curtain. They finish and mill around excitedly as..)*

TINA. Good going everyone, that was really good work – but when we do it for real it's got to be *twice* as good, right? *(to the unseen* **MAN***)* I want to run it again, please.

MAN'S VOICE. *(off)* Whenever you're ready.

TINA. Okay, so just a few points – Lynne, you're still late on the pickup – Rose, you've stopped hiding but you're leaning – Dorothy, watch the arms – Andy – you did great.

(The others show how pleased they are for Andy…and **GEOFFREY** *plants a small kiss on her cheek.)*

(The main curtain comes across.)

*(***MRS. FRASER*** *is entering from the wings with a tray loaded with styrofoam cups of coffee – so that she finds herself stuck, outside the curtain – and a spot hits her as she moves center and tries and fails to get through the curtain. Realizing for the first time that she is being watched by the audience, she jerks her head back haughtily and exits the way she entered.)*

(As she does, the spot goes out and there is a drum roll.)

MAN'S VOICE. Ladies and gentlemen! Due to an unprecedented public response after their appearance here *last* year – we are proud to present the *return* of the Tina Tatowski Tappers!

(And the music strikes up and the curtains open and:)

Scene Twelve

(A year later. The glitzy final tap routine.)

"STEPPING OUT"

COMPANY.

YESTERDAY WAS DULL AND GREY
IT'S TIME TO CHASE THOSE CARES AWAY
BY STEPPING INTO THOSE DANCING SHOES
AND STEPPING OUT OF THE BLUES

NEVER MIND THE DAILY GRIND
IT'S TIME TO LEAVE THAT FAR BEHIND
JUST PUT YOUR WORRIES BACK ON THE SHELF
YOU'RE STEPPING OUT OF YOURSELF

SHIMMERING TIGHTS AND GLIMMERING LIGHTS
THAT SPARKLE AND GLOW
GLITTER AND LACE – THAT LITTER THE PLACE
MEAN DOING A SHOW – READY TO GO – SO

TIP YOUR HAT AND TAP YOUR FEET
AND SLAP THOSE RHYTHMS LOUD AND SWEET
NOW HERE'S YOUR CHANCE TO SING AND DANCE
JUST FIND YOURSELF A SMILE
WE'RE STEP STEP STEP STEPPING OUT IN STYLE

(break)

SHIMMERING TIGHTS AND GLIMMERING LIGHTS
THAT SPARKLE AND GLOW
GLITTER AND LACE – THAT LITTER THE PLACE
MEAN DOING A SHOW – READY TO GO – OH

EVERYBODY KNOWS IT'S TRUE
IF WE CAN DO IT SO CAN YOU
LET'S TAKE A CHANCE – SING AND DANCE
BE HAPPY FOR A WHILE
WE'RE STEP – STEP – STEP –
STEP – STEP – STEP –
STEP – STEP – STEP – STEPPING OUT IN STYLE

EVERYBODY KNOWS IT'S TRUE
IF WE CAN DO IT SO CAN YOU
LET'S TAKE A CHANCE – SING AND DANCE
BE HAPPY FOR A WHILE
WE'RE STEP – STEP – STEP –
STEP – STEP – STEP –
STEP – STEP – STEP – STEPPING OUT IN STYLE

The End

COSTUME PLOT

The following is a partial list of costumes – those suggested in the script. Various changes in accessories, outerwear, etc will be helpful in establishing passage of time and the changing of seasons.

I,1:

TINA

    T shirt

    Tights

    Leg Warmers

    Scuffed, well-used tap shoes

    Man's sweater (tied around waist)

MRS. FRASER

    Wool Coat

    Knit hat

    'clumpy' shoes

SHELLEY

    Bright, outrageous clothing

    Old white sneakers

MAXINE

    tight red leotard

    Black turtleneck

    Long red leg warmers

    'big rock' rings

DOROTHY

    black, shiny tap shoes

    Leotard without tights

    White cotton underpants (slightly showing)

    Ace bandage on knee

LYNNE

    leotard

    Tights

    Leg warmers

    Cardigan that matches leg warmers

    Scuffed tap shoes

ROSE

    Obvious wig

    Bright pink dress

Black tights
White tap shoes with mismatched laces (1 short black, 1 short white)
large strings of beads
many rings

ANDY

long cardigan
Plain dress
New tap shoes

VIVIENNE

expensive belted trench coat
High heels
Leather purse
Leotard with sleeves
Stylish short dance skirt
New tap shoes

GEOFFREY

cheap tap shoes with laces

I,2: (All with dance clothes under)

GEOFFREY

overcoat
Muffler
Street shoes or boots
Sports jacket
Bright hand knit multi-colored sweater vest

VIVIENNE

Leather trench coat w/fake fur trim
High polished boots

ANDY

Shapeless coat
Hat
Neck scarf

I,3: (dance clothes under outer wear)

ANDY/GEOFFREY

as above

ANDY

sleeveless blue leotard (duplicate from I,1)

SHELLEY
  short down parka
  Boots
  Add: leg warmers
ROSE
  neat dufflecoat
  Head scarf
  Boots
MAXINE
  chic coat
  Dorothy:
  moonboots
  Heavy pants
  Parka
  Vest w/reflector tape
  Head lamp
  Knapsack
  Purse
  Bike pump
  Dance gear
LYNNE
  Nurse's uniform
  Nurse's shoes
  Bag

I,5:
TINA, MAXINE, SHELLEY, ROSE, DOROTHY
  Street clothes (add skirts, etc)

I,6: All in rehearsal clothes (1 month later)
VIVIENNE
  gold belt
DOROTHY
  bike helmet

I,7:
ANDY/GEOFFREY
  street clothes (after rehearsal)

I,8:

TINA

dance clothes

LYNNE

Nurse's uniform

Rain Slicker

Bag with tap shoes

DOROTHY

Rain gear

VIVIENNE

Street clothes

Change: Silver Cat suit

MAXINE

in bag: Large hooded sweatshirt 'Save the whales'

II,1:

DOROTHY

handknit leg warmers

Matching head band

ROSE

Bandanna

II,2:

GEOFFREY

Raincoat

ANDY

Coat

II,3:

All in rehearsal clothes. Change off to street clothes

II,4:

MAXINE, DOROTHY, ROSE, SHELLEY

Street Clothes

II,5:

TINA

Rehearsal clothes

II,6:

All in rehearsal clothes

    7 hats including: red fez, Stetson, straw boater

II,7

TINA/LYNNE

    Rehearsal clothes

II,8:

    Rehearsal clothes

II,9:

TINA/MRS. FRASER

    As in II,8 (rehearsal clothes)

LYNNE

SHELLEY

MAXINE

STREET CLOTHES

ROSE

DOROTHY

    Street Clothes with bike gear

II,10:

ALL DANCERS

    Striped blazers

    Straw hats (boaters)

ANDY

    Tap shoes dyed black

GEOFFREY

    Suit jacket with pocket for a sheet of Paper

II,11:

MRS. FRASER

    Coat and hat

FURNITURE AND PROPERTY LIST

I,1: GYM - an evening in February

On Stage

> Stage. On it - clutter from community activities: eg. Boxes of children's musical instruments, arts and crafts supplies, gym and sports equipment, scenery pieces from various amateur productions.
>
> Step Unit to stage
>
> Metal folding chairs

On Walls

> Electric Heaters
>
> Light switches
>
> "No Smoking" signs
>
> Children's art work
>
> Bulletin Boards with community notices etc.
>
> Stool with a cushion
>
> Old Upright Piano (practical)
>
> On piano
>
>> Piano music
>>
>> Apple core
>>
>> Small Cashbox
>>
>> Empty juice carton
>>
>> Spiral bound ledger and pen
>>
>> Can of Diet Soda w/straw (practical)
>>
>> Pack of cigarettes and lighter (Tina)
>
> Next to piano
>
>> Metal wastebasket
>>
>> Mrs. Fraser's bag

Personal

> Maxine - Large rings on fingers (throughout)
>
>> Large Tote bag
>>
>> In - red leotard with sleeves blue leotard, sleeveless (duplicate of Andy's In I, 3)
>
> Dorothy - Ace knee bandage
>
> Shelley - Chewing gum (used throughout)
>
> Rose - Beads, rings, wig
>
> Mrs. Fraser - Overcoat, knitted hat
>
> Vivienne - Expensive leather purse
>
>> In - wallet with dollar bills

I,2: Gym Lobby: one month later

On Stage

> Toilet Door sign
>
> Bench

Geoffrey - Sandwich wrapper (eg. Subway)
    Last bites of a sandwich (practical)
    Briefcase
        In - Geoffrey's tap shoes
        Pocket lighter
        Gym key (I,3)
Off stage
    Vivienne - Shopping bag from a recognizable high-end store (eg. Saks, Hermes)
        in - toilet brush
    Totebag
        In - Thermos w/screw off cup
        Hot coffee
        Sugar Packets
    Andy: Tote bag with Tap Shoes

I,3: Gym: one week later
Off Stage
    Rose - Bag with Dance Shoes
        Crucifix on chain
    Shelley - Bag with new red tap shoes
        Gum
    Maxine - Shopping Bag w/ 2 new shirts (packaged)
    Dorothy - Knapsack w/purse, bike pump, headlight, dance gear
    Vivienne - Yellow rubber gloves
        Can of air fresher
        Small zip-loc bag with coasters
        Wastebasket
        Apple
    Tina - Dance Bag with Tap Shoes
    Lynne - Dance Bag
    Mrs. Fraser - Music case
Purse with handkerchief or tissues
(Geoffrey - Gym key)

I,4: Gym Lobby: later the same evening
Dorothy's Bike with a combination lock
Off stage - Dorothy - Bike helmet, knapsack, etc.

I,5: The Dreamaway - later the same evening
On Stage - Small table
    On: 3 near empty wine glasses
    1 near empty beer glass
    1 empty juice glass
    1 empty individual bottle of orange juice
    5 stools or chairs
Tina: Purse or dancebag
Off stage - Tray
    On: 3 glasses of wine
    1 glass of beer
    1 individual bottle or orange juice

I,6: GYM: a month later: (as scene 1)
On Piano - 2 empty cartons of orange juice
    Coke can
    Banana skin
    Sheet music
    Magazine
Wastebasket - In: pack of cigarettes
On chairs
    1. Dirty sock
    2. Vivienne's gold belt
    Coasters
    Andy - Petition on a clipboard, pen
    Tina - Lighter, cellphone
    Shelley - Lipstick
    Rose - Purse or change purse with $5
    Maxine - Hairbrush
    Misc. purses, totes and dance bags

I,7: Coffee Shop: the same evening:
    Booth or table with 2 chairs
    2 Coffee Mugs

I,8: Gym: 2 weeks later:
On stage
    Wastebasket (by piano)
    Tina - unlighted cigarette
        Small notebook
        Purse

Off Stage
>Lynne - Bag
>Dorothy - Bicycle and gear
>Mrs. Fraser - Music case
>Tote bag with magazine
>Maxine - Purse with class money
>>Shopping bag:
>>>In - Large hooded sweatshirt –
>>>'Save the Whales" printed on
>All others - Dance bags with shoes
>>Personal bags, etc.
>>Money for class

ACT II

II, 1: Gym - one week later:
On Stage
>on piano - Tina's cellphone, cigarettes, lighter
>Mrs. Fraser's handbag
>>In - fruit
>>Magazine
>Lynne - Cashbox
>Tina - Dance bag
>Vivienne - Wastebasket
>Shelley - Doughnut, deli bag, gum
>Class - Money
>>Various personal belongings, purses and dance bags

II, 2: Gym Lobby - later that evening:
On stage
>on bench - Vivienne's bag (large enough to add cleaning supplies
> Geoffrey - Keys to gym
Off stage
>Vivienne - Plastic bucket with cleaning supplies

II, 3: Gym: two weeks later
>On stage
>>Tina - Notebook
>>>8 or 9 bamboo canes
>Personal items, dancebags, purses, etc.
>Wastebasket
>>In - Tina's cigarettes

Off stage
     Vivienne - Yellow rubber gloves
          Aerosol air freshener
          Bag
                  In: tape measure
     Geoffrey - Raincoat
          Band aid for finger
Personal
     Tina - Key to Gym

II,4: The Dreamaway, later that evening:
On stage
     Table and stools or chairs from I,5
     4 drinks including 1 sherry (Dorothy)

II,5: Gym Lobby, two weeks later:
Off stage
     Maxine - Cane
          Dance bag w/dance shoes
          Cardboard box tied with string
                  In - 7 hats including:
                  red fez
                  Stetson
                  Straw hat (boater)
Personal
     Tina - cell phone
          Cigarettes and lighter

II,6: Gym, immediately following:
On stage
     Canes for all dancers (Shelley's with white painted end)
     Music and magazine on piano
     Dorothy: Dance bag and box of tissues
     Miscellaneous personal belongings
II,7: Gym Lobby (w/Gym in background), same evening:
Personal
     Tina - Cell phone (from II,6)

II,8: Gym, 2 weeks later
On stage
>Hats from II,5 PLUS ONE (8 hats)
>Canes from II,6
>Wastebasket
>>In - cigarettes
>Miscellaneous personal belongings
>Music and magazine on piano

II,9: Gym, later the same evening:
Off stage
>Dorothy - Cycling gear and helmet

II,10: Gym, 3 weeks later:
On stage
>Maxine - Pile of fishnet stockings
>Vivienne - Straight pins / pin cushion (on wrist?)
>>Purse -
>>>in - small photo album
>Mrs. Fraser - Note pad and pen
>Andy - Bag w/appointment book or PDA
>Lynne - iPod with ear buds
>Dorothy - Purse -
>>In - tissues
>On piano
>>Magazine
>>Can of diet soda (Tina)
>>iPod dock and speakers

Off stage
>Geoffrey - Card table
Personal
>Geoffrey - Sheet of paper
>Andy - Bandage around hand and wrist

II,11: Local auditorium, one week later -
On stage
>8 straw hats (boaters)
Off stage
>Mrs. Fraser - Hand bag
>Hand held microphone
>Tray with cups of 'tea' (not practical)
>styrofoam or paper (can be glued to tray)

II,12 - As previous scene, one year later

SOUND EFFECTS

I,5: Bar ambient sounds (optional)
I,7: Coffee Shop ambient sounds (optional)
I,8: Cell Phone ring
II,3: Car Horn
II,4: Bar ambient sounds (optional)
II,11 Microphone (practical)
      Microphone feedback and distort